Tao

Acknowledgements

I want to thank Kathryn Ross (my agent) for always being so generous with her time and for being so encouraging and dynamic and funny! I am also blessed with three wise and wonderful editors in Caroline Royds, Genevieve Herr and Maya Gartner. Thanks to my mother, Nathalie, for always encouraging me to write ... and for passing on her own flair for words. Thank you, Paul, for allowing me use some of your "colourful" expressions and Anna for your extensive knowledge of all things animal! Last, but most certainly not least, thanks to my lovely wife, Astrid, for listening and indulging and helping sift the dross from the genuine.

Tao

By

John Newman

**WALKER
BOOKS**

First published 2011 by Walker Books Ltd
87 Vauxhall Walk, London SE11 5HJ

2 4 6 8 10 9 7 5 3 1

Text © 2011 John Newman

Cover illustration © 2011 Del Thorpe

This book has been typeset in Slimbach.

Printed and bound in Great Britain by Clays Ltd, St Ives plc

British Library Cataloguing in Publication Data:
a catalogue record for this book is
available from the British Library

ISBN 978-1-4063-3260-5

www.walker.co.uk

For my three children,
Astrid, Frank, Sean.
In no particular order!

Part 1

Chapter 1

The Big Thing: I bet when the *Titanic* hit the iceberg they didn't think anything of it. It's only an itsy-bitsy iceberg, they probably said, nothing to worry about. They thought that it was just a little thing. But they were so wrong! It was a BIG thing.

I didn't think at all about the phone call that I answered on the evening of my tenth birthday. I thought that it was just a wrong number. A little thing. But it wasn't a little thing! It was a BIG thing.

Jo had dropped me home late. Then she drove away. Kalem and David were already waiting impatiently in the hall for me.

"You're late," said David. "Let's go!"

"Go on. Go on," said Kate (that's my mum). "Cake and presents later." She shoved a twenty-pound note into my hand and pushed me towards the door. But then the phone rang and without thinking I picked it up.

"Tao!" shouted David. "We haven't time!" Kalem just sighed. Kalem doesn't get ruffled easily, but David is always freaking out about something.

"Hello," I said.

"Hello," answered a girl. She sounded nervous.

"Who is it?" whispered Kate loudly.

"I don't know," I mouthed. "Who is this?" I said.

"I'm Mimi," the girl said.

I didn't know any Mimi.

"Come on! Let's go!" hissed David. "We'll miss the whole film."

"Sorry, but you've got the wrong number," I told her. "Bye." I put down the phone and ran out the front door with David and Kalem.

"Who was it?" called Kate. "Enjoy yourselves!"

"Someone called Mimi," I shouted back.

And that was it. I forgot about it straight away. I just thought that it was somebody getting a wrong number, but I was the one who was wrong.

Chapter 2

That was the Big Thing … but this was the First Thing: That morning I had jumped out of my bed the minute I woke up … because it was my birthday! Taa daa! Ten years old. And ten is my lucky number. I looked in the mirror. I had grown taller during the night. No doubt about it. Anyone could see that.

Then Kate came in with my present.

"Happy birth— Would you put on some clothes please, Mr Tao? Really! Admiring yourself in the mirror in your knickers at this hour of the day. I know it's your birthday, but still…"

Of course I was not admiring myself in my knickers.

"They are called boxer shorts," I told her and

started pulling on my tracksuit bottoms.

"Well, whatever. Happy birthday. Now give me a birthday hug."

My mum is big into hugs. She hugs everyone, except for Dad, of course. And, this is a bit embarrassing, she sometimes even hugs trees.

"Try it, Tao," she says, her arms around a great big oak. It's a special feeling – to be at one with nature. And the tree feels it too, Tao, right down to its roots."

Sometimes if there is nobody around I give a tree a hug to keep her happy.

"So how does it feel, Tao?" she asks.

"Hard and lumpy," I tell her.

A birthday hug is like an everyday hug multiplied by ten. It's a real squeeze-the-life-out-of-you hug and it goes on for ages, and for special added extras Kate kisses me all over my face and chants, "IloveyouIloveyouIloveyou!"

I doubt if other boys have to put up with this kind of stuff.

Kate had a parcel in her hand, all wrapped up in newspaper with a blue ribbon holding it together. Kate believes in recycling – she says a small forest is probably cut down every month to make wrapping paper that people just rip up anyway in their rush to see what present they've got. So she uses newspaper instead.

"Open it!" she said. "You're going to love it."

I wasn't so sure about that. I still remember the homemade playdough chess set she gave me last year when I was nine. I was supposed to love that too. So I got my smile ready and tore the parcel open.

It was a Wolverhampton Wanderers football shirt – my favourite team. Not bad at all!

"Thank you." I smiled without having to pretend.

"Put it on," she said, so I pulled it over my head and it fitted. It wasn't three sizes too big so I would get years out of it – it was just right.

"It fits!" I laughed.

"Well of course it does," said Kate, "but not for long unless you stay the same size."

I had to tell her that it was too late for that.

"I started my growth spurt last night."

She gave me that funny look that adults give when they don't believe a word you're saying but don't want to say it right out.

"Do I get a kiss then?" she asked, tapping her cheek with her finger. "And a hug?"

So I gave her a kiss and a hug and she nearly squeezed the life out of me.

Then the doorbell rang and I was saved.

The Second Thing: "It's your father," called up Kate in the tired voice she uses to talk about Dad.

"Coming," I shouted, and pulled on my trainers without bothering to tie up the laces.

"Happy birthday, Tao," Dad called out cheerfully as I raced down the stairs. "I'm just dropping in for a minute with your present." He handed me a big wrapped-up box. "Go on, open it. You're going to love it!"

Dad is always sure about things. If he says I'll like it, I probably will. But Kate had to mutter, "That'll make a change."

"Why do you say that?" I snapped at her. "I always love Dad's presents."

She folded her arms across her chest and made her thin mouth. I didn't care. I just ripped off all the wrapping paper and … it was a cage and there was a fat little white mouse standing holding onto the bars and looking right at me, twitching his nose.

"Yes!" I shouted and punched the air. I'd always wanted a mouse, but Kate was afraid of them so that was that. Dad was beaming.

"Happy birthday, son," he said and we high-fived.

"Thankyouthankyouthankyou." I smiled and gave him a quick hug.

But Kate wasn't a bit pleased. She had stepped right back to the other side of the kitchen.

"How could you?" She almost spat the words at

Dad. She looked like she was going to cry. "You know how I feel about rats."

"It's not a rat, Kate," sighed Dad and, turning his back on her, put his little finger between the bars of the cage and petted the mouse's tummy.

"How could you stoop so low?" Kate's voice was getting louder. "Using Tao's birthday to get at me."

"It's not always about you, Kate," said Dad in his cold voice. "Tao's always wanted a pet. He's been asking for ever."

That was true, but now I was just fed up. Stuck in the middle again. Ever since Jo took my Dad away to live with her, I feel like I'm the knot in the middle of the rope in a tug-of-war between my mum and my dad. Pulled this way and that. That's why I hate HER.

"No – it's always about YOU YOU YOU!" yelled Kate. "You are so—"

"But it's never about ME, is it?" I interrupted her. "Even on my birthday!" And wiping the tears off my face with the back of my hand, I picked up the cage and the red envelope that came with it and ran out of the kitchen and up to my room.

The Third Thing: "Well done," I could hear Dad saying in a sarcastic voice. "Another big day ruined for the boy."

"Just go, James," said Kate through her teeth.

The front door closed. Then his car pulled away.

"Welcome to my world, mousey," I told my new pet as I put the cage down on the bed and lay down beside it. Then I blew my nose hard. I could hear Kate downstairs, banging cupboards and clattering cups. I opened the catch on the cage door and slowly reached in my hand. The mouse had moved back into a corner and was very still. Its heart was beating wildly and I could see its whole body quivering.

"It's OK, little mousey," I said quietly. "I won't hurt you." The mouse sniffed at my fingers, its nose twitching. Very gently, I petted its back with my finger. It didn't move away.

"You are the best little mouse," I whispered. His heart was already calming down, but I knew I had to go slowly in the beginning until he got used to me. I pulled my hand slowly back out of the cage and closed the door.

The Fourth Thing: The mouse started sucking on its water bottle. That is, until my mobile phone went off.

ANSWERMEANSWERMEANSWERME, it roared and the mouse ran for cover into its nest of hay. I jumped too. David had downloaded this new ringtone for me and I wasn't used to it yet.

It was a text from Dad.

Glad you liked the
present. I'll pick
you up at 2 outside
Happy Pear

As if nothing had happened. Dad never mentions
rows. Kate says that it's because he doesn't care, but
that's not true. He just wants to forget about them.
Kate never forgets rows.

The Fifth Thing: I opened the red envelope. Inside
was a card that sang Happy Birthday in a squeaky
voice when you opened it and it was signed by Dad.
He wrote, "Welcome to double figures." SHE wrote,
"When I was your age, Tao, I was ... ten!"

"Which SHE probably thinks is very funny, ha ha,"
I told Mousey, who was peeping out of his nest again.
"But I don't. It's a stupid thing to say." Mousey put
his head to one side and looked at me in a funny way.
The twins, Roger and Rachel (who are only two), had
drawn pictures of me with fat crayons. Well, I guess it
was me because SHE had written "Tao – by Rachel"
under the crooked circle with the arms coming out of
the ears and no legs, and "Tao – by Roger" under the
black smudge.

The Sixth Thing: Kate pushed open the door and
stuck her head in.

"Tao?" she said quietly.

I didn't answer her. I was still cross.

"Sorry," she whispered. I could hear in her voice that she had been crying.

"Who is the card from?" she asked, even though she could have easily guessed.

"Dad. And the twins," I told her without looking up.

About now Kate should have crossed the room and tried to hug me and I would pull away for a bit, but then I'd let her and then we'd be friends again. But this time she didn't come any further than the door.

"There's nothing to be afraid of," I said. I still sounded angry. That's because I was. "It's only a little mouse, you know. *It's* the one who should be scared of you."

"I know, I know." Kate braced herself and moved slowly into the room.

"He won't eat you!" I told her and she laughed nervously. Then she sat on the end of the bed as far away from the cage as she could. The mouse stood up holding the bars and looked at her curiously. Kate tensed up. Then she took in a big, deep breath right down to the toenails and let it out slowly. That's one of the calming tricks that she learnt in one of her classes.

"Sorry, Tao," she said again, and because it was my birthday and I really didn't want it spoiled, I let her hug me.

"Sorrysorrysorry," she said, and there was a crack in her voice.

"I'd better go," I said, wriggling out of her arms. "You know Willy isn't to be trusted on his own in the shop."

Kate smiled when I said that. It's what she always says.

Chapter 3

The Seventh Thing: The Happy Pear was quiet when I got there. I parked my bike around the back and went to see where Willy had got to. He wasn't in the shop and there was Mr Kelly waiting patiently at the till with a basket full of vegetables. This was not unusual. Kate had warned Willy about this ... lots of times.

"Someday, someone is just going to stick their hand in the till and take all the money!" she'd yell, throwing her hands in the air.

But Willy would just smile in that big daft way of his and tell her to, "Chill, Kate. You've got to be a more trusting woman. God looks after the good people."

And so far I had to admit he was right. Nobody had

ever put their hand in the till. Still, Kate didn't like to leave him too long on his own and that's why I always worked there on a Saturday, which was her only day off, even though it was my birthday and Kate said that she would skip her yoga and drumming classes today if I wanted the day off. But I didn't want the day off. I love working in The Happy Pear – looking after Willy, who is thirty, and serving all the people that I know and who always stop for a chat.

"Have you been waiting long?" I asked Mr Kelly, and started weighing his bananas.

"Oh, just about fifteen minutes or so. Willy is busy in the café and I'm in no hurry."

I served Mr Kelly and then I went to find Willy.

"Willy!" I shouted.

"In here," he called back from the coffee shop.

Willy was standing on top of the stepladder painting one of his "Willyisms" across the ceiling. He was just about finished.

The words were painted in blue in a spiral shape so you had to walk in a circle to read them.

Don't be too open-minded, I read out loud, bending my neck back, *or your brains might fall out.*

"It's good, isn't it?" said Willy, coming down off the ladder. "I think it's one of my best. The customers will love it. What do you think, Tao?"

"So where did you steal this one from?" I asked.

"Tao!" said Willy in that slow drawl of his. "Of all people to think like that. A boy whose name means 'wisdom'. Wisdom cannot be stolen, Tao, only shared. I saw it written on a T-shirt. Good, isn't it?"

Then he ruffled my hair and said happy birthday and promised me that he'd bring me in a present tomorrow.

"Yeah, yeah, yeah," I said.

He had said that last year too and I am still waiting. He pretended to look hurt and then he ordered me back into the shop because someone could be in there putting their hand in the till and stealing all the money while I was idling away my time in here admiring his work. I wasn't admiring his work, but a lot of customers do come in just to read Willy's Willyisms, which is why Kate doesn't mind him painting them higgledy-piggledy all over the coffee shop.

"And always remember, Tao," Willy called after me as he folded up the ladder, "better to be thirty years young than ten years old!"

Willy and I took our break before the lunchtime rush, when The Happy Pear gets busy, especially on a sunny Saturday like today.

"It is a well-known fact," began Willy, and took

a big bite out of his brown-bread-cheese-and-tomato sandwich, so that I had to wait while he finished chewing it before I could find out the "well-known fact". Willy takes his digestion very seriously and food has to be well chewed before swallowing.

"What was I saying?" he asked when his mouth was finally empty.

"You were talking rubbish as usual," I told him.

"No I was not, young Tao," he said. It was my turn to take a huge bite of my bread roll. "What I was saying was that it is a well-known fact that the pet you choose is the person you are."

"Wha—?" I said, or tried to with my mouth full. Willy brushed the crumbs that I had sprayed off his jumper.

"My personal choice of pet would be a lion," he continued. "Now what does that say about me?"

"You own a cat," I told him, "a fat lazy cat called Winnie."

"Ah, but that's the point," smiled Willy, pointing his sandwich at me. "Cats and lions are first cousins. It is the closest you can get to owning a lion in this country."

"So what does a lion say about you, Willy?" I asked in a sarcastic voice.

"That I am a king among men. A fierce and dangerous carnivore."

"But you're a vegetarian," I reminded him.

"Don't sweat the small stuff, Tao," said Willy, waving his bread about. A slice of tomato went flying but he didn't notice. "The question is, what does a mouse say about you?"

"That I'm cute and I can twitch my nose?" I answered, and twitched my nose.

Willy laughed and took a slurp of his disgusting wheatgrass and turnip juice, which is the drink of choice for lion-men, I suppose. Of course, the juice reminded him of my disaster.

"So Mouseman, have you and your friend Mr Twit destroyed any more kitchens?" he asked.

"Not this week," I said, and wished that I had kept my big mouth shut.

Chapter 4

The Eighth Thing: Last week, Kate gave me a big bag of fruit to take to Kalem's mum, Angela, on my way to training. The fruit was a bit soft and The Happy Pear only sells the freshest of fruit, so every day the stuff that is not sold is thrown out onto the compost heap or given away free to friends. Angela is Kate's best friend. When we go on holidays, Angela helps out in The Happy Pear.

"Kate says you might make a tart with it or something," I told Angela when I handed her the bag of fruit.

"How about a smoothie?" suggested Kalem. "Can Tao and I make a smoothie, Mum?"

"Sure," said Angela. "Just don't make a mess."

So we chucked about half the bag of fruit into the smoothie mixer, then Kalem poured in a carton of apple juice.

"Whizz her up, Tao!" he ordered. So I turned the knob to full.

"Help!" I screamed as smoothie mix exploded out of the top all over the kitchen. Juice splashed everywhere! Bits of bananas and apples and strawberries shot up to the ceiling. I tried to put my hand across the top to stop the stuff coming out, but that only made things worse – the mess squirted out of the sides all over me and Kalem.

"Help, Kalem! Helphelphelp!" I yelled.

Kalem switched off the power just as Angela came rushing in.

At first she said nothing, just looked around at her once lovely kitchen in horror. Then she said,"I thought I told you two not to make a mess!"

"I forgot to put on the lid," said Kalem sheepishly. A strawberry had exploded on his nose.

"Sorry," I said. "We'll pay for the damage." I could feel liquid banana dripping down my face. I licked it as it passed my mouth. It tasted nice, but it wasn't the time to say so.

Well, we didn't have to pay for any damage, but we

did have to do the clean-up. Angela handed us each a roll of kitchen towel and we did our best ... but in the end she did most of the work.

When we were done, Angela used the rest of the fruit to make us a "proper" smoothie. With the top on the mixer this time.

"Taa daa – delicious and nutritious!" she declared and poured me a glass. And it *was* delicious. Kalem had an orange moustache from the smoothie he was drinking, which looked really funny. I had one too.

"Thank you," we shouted to Angela as we rushed off to our match.

"You're welcome, men in moustaches," she called after us.

"Lose the moustaches," said the Head Honcho, which is what we call our coach. His real name is Bert Cartwright but nobody calls him that – not even the adults. "We want the opposition to fear us – not jeer us. To shake in their shoes, to quake in our wake!" he roared at us.

Honestly, I don't understand half of what the Head Honcho says in his team talks but they always work and we go out "with fire in our bellies", believing that we can win ... even though we nearly always lose.

But last week we did win and it was all thanks to me. The Head Honcho said that I was "the hero of the hour"! It was completely accidental, really. Kalem crossed the ball into the box and I tripped, and as I was falling the ball bounced off my head and flew into the top corner of the net. The Head Honcho said afterwards that it was a "textbook header". We had won our first match in ten weeks.

"All thanks to my smoothie!" laughed Angela as Kalem waved goodbye to me at his door.

"And to my great skill!" I called back as I went out the gate.

And ever since I told Willy all about our smoothie disaster, Willy has taken to calling Kalem "Mr Twit".

The Ninth Thing: "Brace yourself, Tao," warned Dad when he picked me up outside The Happy Pear at two o'clock to take me to his new house. "The twins are very excited."

The twins are always excited, so that wasn't going to be any different from usual.

"Did she make you work on your birthday?" Dad asked then.

I didn't like the way he said "she" instead of Kate, so I answered a bit crossly.

"No, she didn't. I wanted to."

"OK. Down boy!" laughed Dad. "Are you happy

with the pet mouse I got you? What have you called him?"

I told him I was, of course, but I hadn't named the mouse yet and was he sure that it was a he?

"Well, that's what the man in the pet shop said," Dad answered, "but apparently it's hard to tell." And he grinned.

Dad parked the car outside the house but I had hardly got out when Jo had opened the door and the twins had started charging down the drive, shouting, "TaoTaoTao" at the top of their voices.

"They've been like excited puppies all day, waiting for the birthday boy," Jo said as Roger tried to wriggle out from under her arm and Rachel pulled me by the hand to show me the cake.

Well, we had to have some cake first because the twins couldn't wait. They blew out the candles the minute Dad had lit them and he had to re-light them and tell them to let me do it ... but, of course, they didn't. Then everyone sang, "Happy birthday, dear Tao, Happy birthday to you" and Roger stuck his fist into the cake.

"Time for presents," announced Jo, pulling him away from the ruins of the cake.

Rachel had got me her favourite Barbie doll and

she promised to mind it for me when I wasn't there.

"That's really nice of you," I grinned as she took the doll out of my hands.

Roger gave me a fire engine. He showed me how to push it and squirt the water to put out the fire, but he wouldn't let me touch it.

"They chose the presents themselves," laughed Jo and handed me her present – a voucher for the sports shop, so I could choose a present for myself too. Then she gave me a quick hug. I made my body stiff and kept my arms by my sides. She is not my mum. Kate isn't really either because I'm adopted, but she is the only mum I ever want. Jo gave herself a little shake and said in a kind voice that made me feel a bit bad, "I also want to give you this ... if you'll take it."

I didn't know what to say, so I just stood and watched while she pulled her bracelet off her wrist, the one she always wears with all the tiny stars and angels and hearts and other little things hanging off it.

"I don't want your bracelet," I said.

What would I do with a bracelet?

"I know that." She smiled and started taking a little silver wolf off the bracelet. "This is what I want to give you – it's a charm."

I didn't understand what she was talking about, so she explained.

"This is a charm bracelet. All these little objects are 'charms' that I've collected since I was a little girl and each one is special in some way."

"Is it valuable?" I asked.

"It is to me."

Which didn't really answer my question.

"It was given to me when I was ten by my grandmother. She got it for me on a trip she made to China. She said it would protect me and it has," she said. "And now that you are ten, and as you are Chinese, I want to give it to you." And she handed me the tiny silver wolf.

"Why?" I asked.

"So it can protect you."

"Against what?"

"Oh, you never know when you might need protection," she smiled. "Hopefully never."

"Shouldn't you give it to someone in your family?" I asked. I didn't really want it.

"I am," she said.

You are not my family, I thought, but I didn't say it. Then she handed me a small envelope and told me to keep the charm in that so that I would not lose it.

"Thanks," I mumbled and stuck the envelope in my pocket. It was a stupid thing to give to a boy. Maybe I should have said that, but just then Dad came into the kitchen so I let it go.

Dad clapped his hands and said, "Let's play pass the parcel!"

That was not such a good idea. When Dad stopped the music, Rachel was holding the big messy parcel. She didn't know what to do.

"Tear off the paper!" I told her. But as soon as she started opening the first wrapping, Roger jumped up and grabbed at the parcel and started ripping it apart. Jo had to pull it off him and Rachel started crying until we all started pulling it apart together, even Dad. There was paper everywhere when we had finished, but Jo had put in three prizes, chocolate bars, so that Roger and Rachel and I all got a prize. Then she switched on the *Mary Poppins* DVD to calm everyone down while she cleaned up the mess and I sat on the couch and watched it with Roger cuddled up on one side of me and Rachel on the other, both with their thumbs in their mouths.

Every Saturday with Rachel and Roger ends up the same – watching *Mary Poppins*. Everyone has their favourite bit. Rachel gets all excited when Mary Poppins starts taking all the things out of her bag that could not possibly fit in it and clicks her fingers. Rachel tries to click her fingers, but of course she can't so I have to click my fingers for her and then she can't understand why magic doesn't happen when I do it.

Roger's favourite bit is the penguin dance. He jumps off the couch and pulls his trousers down around his hips and joins in the penguin dance … and he is much funnier than the penguins in the film. I haven't really got a favourite bit, but I think I know practically every word of every song off by heart now.

When *Mary Poppins* is over, it is almost seven o'clock and time for the twins to say "Nightie night" and for me to get home to meet Kalem and David for party number two.

The Tenth Thing: SHE said that she would drive me home to get out of the house and away from the kids before she went completely out of her tiny mind, but it took ages to get going because she couldn't find her keys. Dad just shook his head and grinned at me.

"Women," he said. "Where would they be without us men?" He was carrying a half-asleep Roger up the stairs.

"Some help you are!" she called back, as she began to root around in the recycling bin.

"Bet you left them in the car," Dad called back in his jaded voice.

He was right, of course.

"The annoying thing is that he is always right!" Jo laughed, as we finally got going. I don't like it when she laughs. It's annoying. But then she took a wrong turn, stalled when the lights turned green and hit the tyres on the kerb. By the time we got there in the end, I was beginning to think that Dad might be right about women drivers.

"See you, Tao. Enjoy the film," she called as I hopped out of the car.

I nearly forgot and smiled and said thanks but Kate had opened the front door so I just said, "Bye".

Chapter 5

The Eleventh Thing: This thing is the *Big Thing* and it's the first thing that I told you about so you don't have to bother reading about it again ... unless you've forgotten or you skipped that bit – then you'll have to go back to page 9.

Chapter 6

The Twelfth Thing: The cinema is only down the road in Stepdon village and so we were there in no time. David was first, of course. He's the fastest and it's always a race. We call him "the Cheetah".

"The Cheetah wins again," he whooped.

"Cheater, more like," said Kalem, who was last, as usual.

"Bad loser, more like," said David, while I paid for the tickets. Kalem and David are my best friends, but they don't always get along so well with each other.

"Kate showed us the rodent," said Kalem while we waited for the film to start.

"Mousey?" I said. "Great, isn't he? Dad gave him to

me for my birthday. Best present ever."

"Mousey!" jeered David. "That's a rubbish name. Call him 'the Rodent' like Kate does. She wouldn't even go into the same room as him. She just pointed."

"Mousey is just what I call him until I think of a good name," I told David.

"How about Mousey Tongue," suggested Kalem and laughed out loud at some joke that only he got. "He was a Chinese guy – like you, Tao."

I might be Chinese, but I never heard of a name like that. David raised his eyes to heaven and twirled his finger on the side of his head to show how mad Kalem was.

"Call him the Rodent," he said. "That's a proper name for a mouse. The Rodent Strikes Back!" he added dramatically.

"The Attack of the Raging Rodent!" I added.

Then the film started and the talk stopped, but the name Rodent stuck.

The Thirteenth Thing: The film was brilliant. There was some really awesome martial arts fighting in it and all the way home David was practising his chops and kicks.

"Hi ...YAA!" he yelled and leapt into the air, his foot outstretched and his hands rigid.

"Hi ...YAAAHOOO!" I yelled and kicked a lamp post.

"That's rubbish, Tao," said David.

David is a bit of an expert at martial arts. He's tried a few different classes, but he hasn't found the right one yet. So far he has a white belt in karate, a white belt in judo and a white belt in kick-boxing.

"And that's got to add up to at least one black belt," he claims.

"It adds up to a whole lot of nothing," says Kalem. David gave him a karate chop on the arm for that, but Kalem didn't even seem to notice.

Back in the house, Kate lit the candles on a big lumpy cake she had made herself. This time I got to blow them out by myself and the boys cheered and David wanted to give me the birthday bumps, but Kalem said they would need more than two to lift me, so I escaped. When we'd eaten about half the cake (it was delicious – the worse Kate's cakes look, the better they taste) and I'd opened my presents (a football – because I needed to practise, said David, and an underwater torch – for the bath, said Kalem) and I'd shown them Rodent, David's dad collected them both and suddenly the house was quiet again.

"Give me a hug and off to bed," said Kate. "By the way, I rang your father when you were at the cinema and he is coming over tomorrow and we're all going to have a chat… But Tao, there's nothing for you to worry about. Good night. Love you."

Nothing to worry about? Easy for her to say. I was tired after my birthday and now I was fed up. I hate it when adults say that there is nothing to worry about because it always means that there is. The last time Dad and Kate had a "chat" with me was to tell me that they were splitting up.

"A chat about what?" I asked, but I didn't really want to know. So when Kate said it could wait until the morning, after I had had a good night's sleep, I didn't argue, I just said good night and went up to bed.

"Night, night," I said to Rodent and lifted his cage onto the floor.

Rodent was obviously not sleepy because he was galloping around his little wheel thing. I watched him for a bit – he looked really intense, like he was practising for the Olympics.

Thirteen things in one day. That was a lot. No wonder I don't even remember nodding off.

Chapter 7

I didn't sleep very well. I kept wondering what was so important that Dad had to come over to "chat" about it. With Kate. They'd probably end up fighting with each other like they always do.

Why is everything always much worse at night? When I woke up in the morning, it all seemed a bit silly. Suddenly I realized what the "chat" was going to be about. They were going to tell me all about sex and babies and stuff. Kalem's parents told him all about it when he turned ten and he told me, but it was hard to follow.

It was probably Kate's idea to have Dad there for "a man-to-man talk". I bet he wasn't that bothered.

He'd just think that Kate was being a drama queen again. I heard Dad's car already pull up and the door open while I was still in bed. He probably wanted to get it over early so he wouldn't be late for his Sunday golf.

"This is going to be so gross," I told Rodent. I wasn't looking forward to it. All that yucky stuff.

I went down to the kitchen. Dad and Kate were already both there, sitting at the kitchen table.

"Sit down, Tao," said Dad. "Your mother and I have something to tell you."

He sounded serious but kind too. He was probably a bit embarrassed – I know I was. Kate was smiling in a lopsided way. I sat down. My face felt red.

"It's OK," I muttered, "you don't have to tell me. I know all about it already."

"You do?" said Dad, turning to Kate, an astonished look on his face.

"Yeah. Kalem told me."

"Told you what?" asked Kate, looking very puzzled.

I really went red then. My face was burning up. Surely she didn't expect me to explain it back to her.

"You know," I mumbled, "where babies come from … and how they get inside the mummy and all that stuff."

Kate looked at Dad and he looked at her … and

suddenly they both burst out laughing. That was not what I had expected. They never did that. Even before Jo took Dad away from us.

"Oh, Tao," said Kate, still half laughing and ruffling my hair, "we don't want to talk to you about the birds and the bees!"

I jerked my head away.

"Who said anything about birds and bees?" I was cross now.

"You got the wrong end of the stick there, Tao," said Dad, smiling. "That talk is for another day. Now let's get to the matter at hand," he continued, glancing at his watch.

"Can't you miss your damn golf for once?" said Kate and suddenly it seemed like they were about to start one of their rows.

"Then what DO you want to talk to me about?" I put in quickly to distract them. I was really confused by now.

"You got a phone call last night from a girl named Mimi," said Dad, looking straight at me.

"It was a wrong number," I said.

"No, it wasn't," said Dad. "Mimi is your sister."

Kate jumped up.

"You can't just blurt out something like that," she shouted at Dad, "without explaining a thing."

"Well, you explain it then!" Dad shouted back, his eyes blazing.

"What do you mean – 'my sister'?" I asked quietly. I suddenly felt dizzy.

Kate and Dad stopped arguing and looked at me. Kate sat down and put her hand over mine. Dad pulled up his chair and repeated, "You have a sister, Tao. She's Chinese like you and her name is Mimi. She lives in Ireland."

"I know this is a bit of a shock, Tao," said Kate softly.

It was more than a bit of a shock. I felt like being sick.

"She was adopted before you were adopted. By an Irish family. Then they were contacted by the orphanage again—"

"How old is she?" I asked before Kate finished. I didn't understand anything of what she was saying anyway.

"Well…" began Kate, and she looked across at Dad.

But I had another question before they could explain.

"How long have you known about this?" My voice was getting louder now. "When were you going to tell me? You should have told me about this!" I shouted at them and stood up so fast that my chair fell backwards onto the floor with a bang. Then I ran out of the room. Dad tried to stop me, but I yanked my arm out of his hand and ran up the stairs and threw myself on my bed. I wasn't crying, but I was very cross. Very, very cross. My face was in my pillow and my eyes felt so hot that it wouldn't have surprised me if they had burnt two holes in it.

Rodent looked at me through the bars, but I was too angry to explain.

"Well done!" I could hear Kate saying in a sarcastic tone.

And then Dad's sharp, angry answer.

"Well, you handle it then if you're so bloody clever!" The front door slammed and a minute later Dad's car pulled away sharply with a screech of tyres.

Then the phone rang.

Chapter 8

The phone rang five times before Kate, with a loud sigh, picked it up.

"Yes?" I heard her say.

Then, "Oh."

Then, "Mimi?"

I sat up and listened very carefully.

"I don't think this is the best moment," Kate said slowly. "If you give me your number, he'll ring you back. Is your father there?"

I jumped up and ran to the top of the stairs. "Don't hang up!" I shouted down to Kate. "I want to talk to her." I charged down the stairs two steps at a time.

"This is Tao now," Kate managed to say before

I grabbed the phone out of her hand.

"Tao?" said a voice very shyly on the other end. Before I answered, I stared hard at Kate and she understood me well enough because she held up her hands and backed into the kitchen, closing the door behind her.

"Hello, Mimi," I said and suddenly I went all shy too. I didn't know what else to say. Mimi didn't talk either and there was a long silence. Then I could hear some loud whispering.

"Say something, Mimi! Don't just stand there like an eejit with your mouth hanging open." It was a girl's voice. "Ask him who he is and why our dad has his number," she continued.

"OK, Sally!" Mimi whispered back sharply. "Tao, my sister Sally wants to know, and I want to know too, who you are and why my dad has your phone number and why does he say in a letter that's all crumpled up in the waste-paper basket that he thinks it's high time that Mimi and Tao were told the truth?"

She was talking very fast now, all the words tumbling out. If Mimi had a sister, was she my sister, too? I was getting very confused.

"My dad says that you are my sister," I interrupted.

There was another long silence then.

"What did he say?" whispered Mimi's sister in the background.

"He says he is my sister," giggled Mimi.

"That's not what I said – I said that my dad says that you are my sister, and that I am your brother," I tried to explain but it was hopeless.

"Well, whatever," said Mimi. "I think your dad is joking because I already have a brother called Conor. You can ask Sally."

"He isn't joking, Mimi," I said. "I am your brother too."

Kate had come back quietly out of the kitchen and was mouthing that I should put her on the phone. My head was in a spin. I handed her the phone and she asked Mimi if she could speak to her father. But it seemed that Mimi didn't want to get her father. So Kate had to insist. There was a long wait then, with Kate just holding the phone.

Eventually Mimi's father must have come, and Kate and he talked for a very long time. I went out in the garden and kicked the football back and forth against the wall of the house until Kate finally called me in.

I sat down at the table with a long face. I didn't really feel that cross anymore, just fed up and sulky.

"I gave Mimi's dad your mobile number to give to

her," said Kate, putting a glass of water on the table in front of me. "I hope you don't mind?"

I just shrugged. I was surprised that Kate even knew my number.

"It'll make it easier for you to chat in private," she said.

"S'pose so," I mumbled, but right now I didn't really care.

"It's true then – what Dad said – this Mimi is my sister?" I asked her, a bit grumpily. "When exactly were you going to tell me?"

Kate sighed. "Your father and I only found out about Mimi after we had adopted you. Mimi is Chinese, like you. When Rose and Paul, that's Mimi's parents, adopted her from the orphanage in China, they were told that she was an only child. When we adopted you a few weeks later we were told the same thing, but it was a mix-up. Later on, somebody in the orphanage found the papers saying that you were really twins…"

"Twins!" I spluttered. This day was getting stranger and stranger.

"Well, yes," said Kate, "apparently. So they wrote both families a letter, but it was too late then. We weren't going to give you to Rose and Paul, and they weren't going to give Mimi to us."

"When were you going to mention this little thing?" I said in a sarcastic voice. "I think I had a right to know about this!"

I could feel my eyes welling up.

"We were going to tell you both when you were seven."

"But you didn't!"

"Well, no, we didn't," said Kate softly, "because that's when your father and I broke up and it was all upsetting enough without this on top of everything. So we told Rose and Paul to wait for another year or two."

"But that was three years ago," I told her.

"I know, Tao." Kate was biting the corner of her lip. "But then something terrible happened. Mimi's mother, Rose, was run over by a bus when she was out cycling and she died. So we wrote to Paul and said that we would wait until the time was right for Mimi before we said anything..."

"Oh," I said. "That's very sad."

"Yes," said Kate and I didn't push her away this time when she put her arm around me.

"And then Mimi found our phone number and a letter," I finished.

"Her father, Paul, had started to write to us. He hadn't been happy with the letter that he had written so he had crumpled it up and thrown it in the waste-paper basket. Mimi's sister Sally found the letter and she put Mimi up to ringing you yesterday. Mimi didn't know about you before that."

There was a long silence in the kitchen when Kate finished talking and even though I had a lot of questions I didn't want to ask anything else. Sometimes you can have an information overload. I have a twin, was all I could think. I have a twin.

In the afternoon, I met Kalem and we went to play our football match. Angela had made another smoothie for us, as last week it had brought us such luck. It didn't work so well this week.

Questions about Mimi kept popping into my mind. How could you have a twin sister for ten years without knowing about her? What did she look like? Was she taller than me? Because that would be embarrassing. How did she feel about discovering she had a twin? What were Sally and Conor like? Would we meet each other? That was a scary thought.

I didn't say anything about all this to Kalem and he didn't seem to notice anything odd about me on the way to the football field. Actually, I don't think that he would have noticed if the sky had fallen. All he could talk about was his latest bird-brained invention – a whirly washing line powered by some sort of solar-panelled gadget that spun it around when it wasn't windy. I didn't pay him much attention – I had my own thoughts to occupy me.

Even when the match started, I couldn't concentrate. The Head Honcho wasn't too pleased. At half-time he let me have it.

"Tao Clarke, you are not at the races! Wakey wakey! You are running around that pitch like a headless chicken. Matches aren't won by headless chickens! Step up to the plate, man, for God's sake. Take the game by the tonsils – show us some of the va-va-voom that we saw from you last week. I've seen grannies play better!"

But I wasn't much better during the second half, even though Dad arrived to cheer me on. He was there just in time to see me score an own goal. I sort of forgot which direction I was playing for a moment and, for once, kicked the ball really well ... but into the wrong goal.

"TAO!" roared the Head Honcho, flinging the water bottle he was holding onto the ground.

I was substituted soon afterwards. I thought that Dad would not be pleased, but instead he put his arm around my shoulder and said, "Never mind, son. There are more important things than football."

"What's more important than football!" interrupted

the Head Honcho, who was standing close by and throwing his hands towards heaven.

"Some things are, Bert," laughed Dad, and he told me to get dressed and he would drop me home.

When we stopped outside the house, Dad asked me if I wanted to talk, but I didn't and he didn't push it – just said to ring him when I felt ready.

After dinner, I watched TV with Kate. A few times she looked at me in a funny way, but she didn't mention Mimi either. Later on, as I sat up in bed, I could hear her talking about me to Angela on the phone. "He needs to digest it, the poor thing," I heard her say. "It's a lot for anyone to take on board. He'll say something soon, I'm sure."

Rodent had let me pick him up and I was holding him very carefully, just tight enough so he wouldn't jump out of my hands but loose enough so I wouldn't hurt him.

"A new mouse and a new sister in one day," I told him quietly. "All I wanted was a mouse."

"When we first told him that he was adopted, years ago now, he behaved just the same way," Kate was saying. "He was quiet for days and then all the questions came pouring out. That's just Tao's way!"

You can hear everything in our house. Dad used to say that the walls are made of spit and paper, which isn't true, but they must be thin because I can always hear Kate clearly when she is on the phone, even when she whispers.

"What if she doesn't like me?" I told Rodent, "or if I don't like her?" Rodent's heart was beating very fast against my hand. "Don't be scared, little mouse," I whispered. But I knew how he felt because I was a bit scared of Mimi... Just like Kate was scared of Rodent, which was silly but she just couldn't help it.

Just then my phone started shouting in its deep voice, ANSWERMEANSWERMEANSWERME... Rodent got a big fright and wriggled right out of my hands and jumped off the bed and raced straight back into his cage.

It was a text message from a number that I did not recognize.

> Nite nite twin bro.
> Sleep tite nd dnt let
> d fleas bite. Mimi
> XXX

I smiled and texted her back.

> Nite nite twin sis.
> Tao ☺

Then I said, "Sorry about that" to Rodent, who was hiding in his straw, and I closed the cage door. I switched off my light. But I didn't fall asleep for ages. I wondered, was my new twin sister lying awake as well? With a hundred questions racing through her head? Was she a bit scared too? But excited at the same time?

Chapter 9

ANSWERMEANSWERMEANSWERME my phone started yelling again at breakfast.

"Who on Earth is that?" Kate shouted, jumping up.

"My phone." I laughed.

It was another text from Mimi. Attached was a photo of herself taken by Sally. She was dressed in a navy school uniform and she didn't look very tall. She had long black hair and a small face with a very big smile.

> Dis is a pic of me,
> Mimi. Sally took it.
> Mimi XXX

I showed it to Kate. She thought Mimi looked cute and that her smiling eyes showed a cheerful heart. Kate said that even in the photo Mimi exuded a light and pure energy. Does anyone else's mother talk like this? She said that Mimi and I had the same nose.

"That's impossible," I said.

Kate told me not to be so literal, whatever that means. Then she took my photo and I sent it to Mimi.

ANSWERMEANSWERMEANSWERME

Mimi's second message was a photo of Sally. She was eating her breakfast and was looking quite cross, as if she wasn't pleased to have her photo taken. She had very black hair and black eyes and black lips and even black fingernails. She had about four earrings in one ear.

> Dis is my sis Sally.
> Take away all d black
> muck n shes quite
> pretty. Sally says u
> have my nose. Give
> it back at once! Mimi
> XXX

"Oh my!" laughed Kate when I showed her Sally. "She does look a bit fierce!"

I sent Mimi a photo of Kate clearing the table. Kate

wasn't too pleased about that.

"You should at least have waited until I had brushed my hair. I look a mess!"

"It's your inner-self that counts – not your hair," I told her and she gave me a dirty look.

ANSWERMEANSWERMEANSWERME

"Does it have to make that racket?" asked Kate, who still jumped every time Mimi sent a text.

"'Fraid so," I said.

Kate sighed. "I'm not sure I believe you," she said, but I just grinned at her. This time it was a photo of Conor.

> Dis is my big bro
> Conor. He says hi.
> I hav 2 bros now. I
> can't believe it. Mimi
> XXX

Conor looked very big. Was he my brother too, I wondered, but I didn't ask Kate. She was trying to get me to get a move on for school.

"You could do with brushing your teeth too, young man," she said, clearing away my place. "You are going to miss your bus!"

Then the phone piped again.

ANSWERMEANSWERMEANSWERME

"It's driving me mad," shouted Kate, her hands over her ears.

"It's a photo of her dad," I told her and showed her the phone.

> A pic of my dad. He
> says hi. Got 2 go
> now or I'll miss my
> bus. Cya. Mimi XXX

He looked friendly, but older than my dad. Kate looked at that photo for quite a long time.

"Umm," she said, and handed me back the phone as I left the house. Kalem was waiting impatiently at the gate. "By the way, your sister is a rotten speller!" Kate called after me cheerfully.

"No, she's not," I shouted back. "That's text spelling."

"Your sister can send texts?" said Kalem, with a very puzzled face.

"Hold that face!" I told him and photographed him quickly.

> Pic of Kalem best
> friend and weirdo.
> Tao 😊

David had kept a seat for me on the bus. Kalem sat on the seat across from us and told David that I had gone barking mad.

"Tell me something new," said David, and he punched me in the arm, which is his way of saying hello.

"He's getting texts from his sister," continued Kalem.

I laughed, but said nothing. It was fun to keep them guessing.

"Oh, yeah?" sneered David. "So Rachel can text now. Impressive for a two-year-old!" He shook his head slowly from side to side and let out this low whistle through the gap in his front teeth. It was David's way of showing he was impressed.

"The texts are not from Rachel. They are from Mimi," I said.

"Oh? Where did I hear that name before?" wondered David, suddenly showing more interest.

"Hold that face," I said and took his photo, but he put his hand out to block it just at the wrong time. I sent Mimi the photo anyway – which wasn't easy because David was trying his best to grab the phone off me and if we weren't careful, Sam, the grumpiest driver in the world, would kick us off the bus.

David

was all I managed to write.

Ten seconds later my phone yelled again.

ANSWERMEANSWERMEANSWERME

It was a photo of a girl with brown hair and glasses and a big grin.

> My best friend Orla.
> She says David will
> live til hes 90 n hav
> an interesting love
> life. She's weird.
> Mimi XXX

I showed that to David, who was as puzzled as I was – Kalem said he got it, but he said he wouldn't explain it until he got some answers first.

So when we got off the bus, I told them all about my long-lost Chinese sister.

"She's my twin. There was a mix-up in the orphanage in China and she went to a family in Ireland and I came here," I explained. It was strange to be saying all this as if it was nothing much really, when in fact it was the biggest thing that had ever happened in my life … so far.

"Wow," said Kalem. "And how come you only just found out?"

"My parents didn't tell me when I was seven because they were too busy having their divorce," I explained. I felt like I was outside my body, listening to myself talking as if it all had nothing to do with me.

"Then they didn't tell me the next year, or Mimi – that's her name by the way…"

"We know that," interrupted David.

"…because her mother got killed by a bus and she was too upset," I continued.

"Wow!" said Kalem. "I mean, that's sad."

"Anyhow, her sister Sally—"

"She has a sister?" put in David.

"Yes!" I said impatiently. "And a brother, Conor. Let me get on with the story."

"Are they Chinese too?" David wanted to know.

"Let him get on with the story!" Kalem shouted.

"No, they are Irish," I told David, who looked very confused, so I showed him their photos on my phone. He laughed when he saw Sally.

"She's a vampire, Tao," he said. "Keep away from her or she'll bite your neck and suck your blood and you'll be a vampire too, for ever more."

"Can I get on with the story now?" I asked him. "Sally, the vampire, found a letter that her father was writing to Kate all crumpled up in the waste-paper basket and it had our number on it, maybe he had decided to ring up instead. So Sally made Mimi ring the number. But we were rushing out to the cinema and I thought it was a wrong number..."

"That's where I heard the name Mimi before!" shouted out David as if he had won a prize. "I knew it. I just knew it!"

"Well done, David," drawled Kalem in his most sarcastic voice. "The Brain of Britain does it again."

David went quiet for a minute, but then another hare-brained idea rushed into his head and he had to blurt it out. "Maybe she is just pretending to be your sister. She claims that she's your sister ... to get all your money. In your will! You'd better be careful, Tao. This Mimi could be a very clever con artist."

David was very pleased with himself for working all this out, so it was disappointing for him when I said, "What money? I don't have any money."

Kalem just sneered at him and said David was watching too much rubbish on television and he should get his head examined.

I had to turn off the phone in school or else have it confiscated and I suppose that it was the same for Mimi because when I turned it back on after school there was only one text with a photo of a big bottom.

> My teacher Ms
> Hardy's bum. Orla
> took dis pic with my
> fone. Lucky she was
> not cot or we wud
> both b ded. Mimi XXX
>   WTF!!

I wished I had been brave enough to photo my teacher Mrs Piggott's bottom, but if I had been caught my phone would have been confiscated for a week.

"That's one big bum!" said David when I showed him the pic.

"Even Mrs Piggott couldn't compete with that," I agreed and we both laughed.

My phone went again when I was walking home with Kalem and David.

> Dis is a pic of Emma
> my cousin wiggling
> her ears. Mimi XXX

Kalem and David stopped to look at the photo of Emma. Kalem looked at the photo for quite a long time, until David started teasing him saying that he fancied Emma. I was really glad that we had arrived outside The Happy Pear because I was getting sick of the two of them.

"See you tomorrow," I called and ran in to find Kate. Kate usually stops work when I arrive after school and we walk the rest of the way home together.

Before we headed home, I sent Mimi pics of The Happy Pear and of Willie juggling oranges. Then my credit ran out, but Kate said she would buy me more as it was important to show Mimi a slice of my life.

Mimi must have had lots of credit because for the rest of the day texts with pics attached kept on coming. She sent me pics of her dog, Sparkler, her bedroom and her Aunt M (who looked very pregnant).

M for Marigold

she wrote.

She sent a pic of her grandad's car. She called it the jalopy. Her grandad was standing beside it. I don't know who looked older – the jalopy or the grandad. Her grandmother was very fat but she looked jolly. There was someone called Nicholas on a motorbike but he was hard to see because of his helmet. And lots more that I can't remember.

I sent her a pic of me holding Rodent but you could

hardly see him because Kate took the pic and she stood miles away.

"Use the zoom," I said, but Kate couldn't work that out at all.

> My pet mouse
> Rodent

I texted her and pushed "send".
Mimi texted back,

> Looks like blob of ice
> cream on ur jumper.

So I sent her another one of Rodent in his cage and a pic of my bedroom and my house and my garden and I texted her about Rachel and Roger and said that I would send her pics of them tomorrow when I saw them.

That night when I went to bed, Kate rang Mimi's dad and they talked for a long time. I could only make out a few words here and there because it was so windy outside. I didn't really care anyway. I was too tired and there were too many thoughts in my head. I texted Mimi,

Nite, nite 😊

and she texted me,

> Nite nite sleep tite n
> dnt let d bugs bite
> Mimi XXX

and suddenly I felt glad that Mimi was my sister, even though I hadn't even met her.

"I think that you're going to like her," I told Rodent as I slipped him back into his cage. He made straight for his wheel. Night-time was clearly exercise time for my mouse, but I fell asleep straight away.

Part 2

Chapter 10

Kate and Mimi's dad, Paul, made all the arrangements so that Mimi and I could finally meet up.

The plan was that Dad and I would fly over to Dublin together at Easter, which was only two weeks away, so that he could meet Mimi and her family. Dad would only stay a day because he had already arranged to go on a golfing trip to Scotland, which Kate said showed exactly where his priorities lay. We would stay in a hotel because Dad said that it would be too much too soon to stay in Mimi's house, even though her dad said that it was perfectly all right by him. Kate said that we were being downright rude not staying with them. But Dad had made up his mind, so that was that.

Then I would stay for two nights on my own with Mimi's family (which secretly really scared me), until Kate flew over to collect me and she would stay for the Easter weekend before we flew home again. Kate would stay in their house as well, because she had no intention of insulting the Roches by refusing their kind invitation. Willy would just have to manage The Happy Pear on his own!

"So are you very excited to be seeing Mimi at last?" Jo asked me a week before going.

She shouldn't have said the Mimi word because Roger heard her and started shouting, "MIMIMIMIMIMI-MIMIMIMIMIMIMIMIMIMIMIMIMI…" like a machine gun and then Rachel joined in, "MIMIMIMIMIMIMIMIMI-MIMIMIMIMIMIMIMI…" and they both charged around the kitchen table with their arms out like aeroplanes.

"Because," Jo shouted, with her hands over her ears, "if you are even half as excited about Mimi as these two … then you are overexcited!"

Actually I was more terrified than excited, but I wasn't going to tell *her* that. What if Mimi didn't like me … or I didn't like her? Kate said that that wasn't very likely because we were getting on so well by text, but text isn't the same as real life and any time that we had actually talked on the telephone, it had been awkward and we hadn't known what to say to each other. Kate said that that was just shyness and perfectly understandable.

"Twins have a special connection," Jo continued even though I hadn't said a word. "Just look at Rachel and Roger. They are like peas in a pod. Even when they are asleep they both curl up the same way and both suck their thumb on one hand and twist their hair with their little finger on the other hand. You've seen them, Tao, haven't you?"

Of course I had seen them both asleep but I didn't bother answering her, just pretended I was dead interested in the stupid show that was on the TV. She was right though – if you didn't know the twins, you wouldn't be able to tell them apart. But Mimi and I had been separated almost since birth and lived in different families and even in different countries.

"Well?" she said, because sometimes she just won't give up.

"Kate says I talk gobbledygook in my sleep but I bet Mimi doesn't," I told Jo because sometimes I forget that I hate her.

She laughed at that.

I nearly told her that Mimi often talks gobbledygook when she's awake, but I didn't. Yesterday, she texted me that although Sally might look black, she is really green. That was complete gobbledygook to me.

It seemed that all anyone could talk about was Mimi this and Mimi that. When I worked in The Happy Pear on Saturday morning, even the customers knew about her.

"So, young man," Mrs Crowe said as I weighed her broccoli, "Willy tells me that you have recently acquired a twin. A girl twin, no less! You must be a very excited young man indeed." She pinched my chin and clucked like a hen. I hate it when adults do that but mostly I hate the way Willy can't keep his big mouth shut.

"Willy, you are one big big-mouth," I told him, "blabbing about my private life to everybody that steps inside the shop."

"Ah, Tao," he answered with a pretend sad face, "don't be like that. The customers have a right to know, after all."

"No, they don't!" I said crossly, but he just laughed. He had even written another Willyism under the window especially for me.

In the cookie of life, a sister is the chocolate chip.

"Where did you get that one from, Lionman?" I asked him when I had read it.

"Tao," he drawled in his pretending-to-be-hurt voice, "big cats have big thoughts."

"Copy cats, you mean?" I teased him.

Willy grabbed me and put my head in an armlock. He squashed a twenty-euro note into my mouth, so that I could buy him something nice in Ireland. Then he let me go.

"Don't eat it, Mouse," he said as I took the note out of my mouth and tried to flatten it. "That's the money they use in Ireland."

"It looks like Monopoly money," I said, turning it over in my hand.

"Well, give back then!" said Willy, and tried to grab it but I was too quick for him this time.

David helped me prepare for the trip by talking in an Irish accent ... all the time. He was driving me mad.

"Begob Tao, ye'll be thanking me when ye go over der to de land of de leprechaun 'cos, begob boy, dey shure talk funny over der," he told me.

"That's a rubbish Irish accent," I laughed. "Mimi doesn't sound anything like that."

"Well, boy," he laughed, "dat's 'cos de gurl is Chinese-Irish."

Kalem sighed loudly and shook his head.

"In Ireland, they wouldn't call you an idiot, David," he said.

"What would they call me?" asked David suspiciously.

"They'd call you an eejit."

* * *

Even the Head Honcho had something to say.

"Give my regards to U2 when you go to Ireland," he told me, which really made no sense.

"Who to?" I said.

"U2. Bono. Adam. The Edge."

I do wonder about the Head Honcho. Is he sane?

"OK," I said, because sometimes it is safer to agree.

"And Father Ted if you see him," he shouted after me and laughed loudly.

On Saturday, I took Rodent over to Jo's house. She was going to mind him while I was in Ireland. I wasn't too pleased about that, but Kalem couldn't take him because his mum would have a fit if he brought a mouse into the house and David was going away for Easter too.

Before I took him over, I tried to explain to Rodent that it would only be for a few days.

"Robert and Rachel can be a bit hyper," I told him and tickled his fat little tummy, "so just hide in your straw. But if Jo bothers you, bite her."

The twins were very excited about having a mouse to stay over and I was afraid they would terrify poor Rodent, but Jo made them stand back from the cage when I put it on the table.

"May I hold him?" she asked me straight away, which surprised me so much I just nodded. She opened the cage door and put her hand straight in. Kate would have fainted. Jo left her hand very still in the cage with her palm up for a few minutes while Rodent sniffed about and then, I could hardly believe it, he climbed onto her hand!

"I used to have gerbils when I was your age," she said as she lifted Rodent out of the cage. "He's a friendly little fella, isn't he?" she smiled.

"Yes," I said. I wasn't sure how happy I was that he went to her so easily. Robert had come over now and she was showing him how to pet Rodent very gently. Rachel still hung back, but she was very curious.

Dad had stepped into the kitchen. "Your mouse will be in good hands here," he told me. "Jo has a way with animals. Don't you, love?" he said to her.

"Kate is getting used to him," I said.

"Yeah, well..." he muttered.

"Here. You take him," Jo said then, and passed Rodent into my hands. "Rachel can help me fill up his food tray."

Before I left with Dad on Sunday morning, Kate put ten herbal anti-stress drops on my tongue to keep me calm. She made me promise to ring her as soon as

I had arrived and told me a hundred times that there was nothing for me to be nervous about. That everything was going to work out just fine.

"Now, don't be silly about coats," she told me. "It's always raining in Ireland."

"I won't be silly about coats," I told her.

"And if you are upset in any way, or feel sick, or maybe don't like the food or there's anything at all that doesn't feel right, then you must tell Mimi's father straight away … or ask to ring me. But that won't happen, I'm sure."

"I won't get upset," I told her.

"Of course you won't," she said. "I just know that you are going to have a great time … and that's why I'm not one bit worried about you and anyway I'll be there in just a few days' time…" And then she hugged me again so tightly that I was nearly crushed.

"IloveyouIloveyouIloveyouIloveyou," she repeated over and over again as she said goodbye while Dad waited impatiently in the hallway for me to come.

I think Kate was the one who needed the drops.

Chapter 11

It wasn't a long flight. Although it was very smooth, I felt like throwing up all the way.

"It's just nerves," said Dad. "Once you get the first meeting with Mimi over with, you'll be fine."

He squeezed my knee and smiled, then went back to reading his newspaper.

"I need to go to the toilet," I told him, standing up.

"Again?" He threw his eyes to heaven and moved his legs so I could get past him.

Inside the airport, my blue suitcase was the first one on the conveyor belt. I had been hoping that it would take ages or maybe not come at all, but it was the first. Dad only had hand-luggage, so that meant there was no more reason to wait around.

"Come on, son," said Dad, lifting my bag off the belt, "time to face the music."

"Do we have to?" I asked, but Dad just smiled and, putting his hand on my back, pushed me gently towards the Arrivals door.

There were a lot of people in the Arrivals area. Some of them held up signs with names on them. The first name I saw on a sign was TAO. Mimi's father, Paul, was holding it. Dad saw the sign at the same time.

"Over there," he said, pointing.

Mimi was holding her father's hand. They hadn't spotted us yet. She was looking all around and she was biting her lip. Her other hand was a tight fist by her side. Her knuckles were white. I had not thought about Mimi being nervous to see me.

"Come on, Tao," said Dad, because I had stopped walking when I saw her. My arms were tingling and I could feel my hair. Then Mimi saw me.

"Tao!" she called out and tugged her father's sleeve. Then he saw us and his face broke into a big smile.

My dad and Paul shook hands.

"Hello, Mimi," I said, and held out my hand.

Mimi looked at my hand for a moment. She did not seem sure what to do.

"Hello, Tao," she whispered at last and suddenly she threw her arms around me in a big hug, which I wasn't expecting. She nearly knocked me over. Both our fathers laughed and when Mimi let me go she was smiling too.

"Hello, Tao," said Paul and hugged me as well, my face pressed against his stomach. Dad was shaking Mimi's hand and telling her that she was a beauty.

Then everyone seemed stuck for words for a moment, until Paul said, "Right let's go, because there are a lot of people waiting to meet you, Tao."

The adults led the way to the car and Paul explained to Dad that, although the whole family had wanted to come to the airport to meet us, they had decided that it might be a bit much at one go for poor Tao.

"You would probably have turned on your heel and headed straight back home!" he said to me as he put his parking ticket in the machine.

Mimi and I walked along behind. She glanced at me a few times and smiled shyly, but we didn't say anything to each other. My mouth was dry and I couldn't think of what to say. Mimi must have felt the same. My hands felt sticky.

It was the same in the car. Mimi and I sat on each side of the back seat, the empty middle seat between us. Our dads were in the front talking away, the way adults do. Paul was explaining the itinerary – whatever that was.

"First you get to meet the rest of the family, Conor and Sally, and that's going to be pretty scary, Tao." And he laughed.

"He's not worried about that," put in my dad. But he was wrong.

"Oh yes I am," I said, and Paul smiled and told me that I would be fine. One part of me wished that I had stayed at home.

"That's the Dublin Mountains ahead," pointed out Paul. "We live behind those mountains, Tao. Isn't that so, Mimi?"

Mimi looked at me and made a funny face, as if to say that she hadn't got a clue and I couldn't help giggling a bit. I do that sometimes when I'm nervous.

"If the traffic stays light, we'll be home in about forty minutes, I'd say," continued Paul. "What do you reckon, Mimi?"

Mimi made the same funny face again and shrugged her shoulders. I put my hand over my mouth to stop the giggle.

"That's roughly about what it takes for us to get to the airport as well," added Dad. "Am I about right, Tao?"

This time it was my turn to make a funny face and shrug my shoulders to show Mimi that I hadn't got a clue … and her turn to put her hand over her mouth and giggle.

"What's the big joke, you two?" asked Paul, moving out a lane to pass a lorry.

We both burst out giggling then, although there wasn't really anything much to laugh about.

"They're twins, all right!" said Dad, and both he and Paul laughed.

"Emma, that's my cousin," said Mimi, out of the blue, "you'll meet her soon because she says she can't wait to meet you and she'll be over like a shot when we get home … well, she's a terrible giggler, isn't she, Dad?"

"She's the world's worst," laughed Paul. "When she starts there is no stopping her and if she gets a fit when she's eating or drinking, it's a total disaster!"

"It all comes squirting out of her nose," added Mimi.

"Tao's mother, Kate, has an extraordinary laugh too," joined in my dad. "When she gets a fit of laughter, she starts snorting! It's quite embarrassing actually."

"No, it's not," I interrupted him crossly. "It's funny." I didn't like him talking about Kate in that way to strangers.

There was an awkward silence in the car for a moment after that … and *that* was embarrassing!

Then Dad said, "Of course. You're right. It is funny."

He turned his head and smiled a sorry at me.

"I can't wait to hear her snort," said Mimi. Everyone laughed and that cleared the air.

"Nearly there," said Paul. "Mimi's grandparents live up that road." He pointed up a road lined with trees as we drove by.

I looked across at Mimi and she smiled and suddenly unbuckled her seat belt and moved into the middle seat beside me for the rest of the journey.

She clicked in her seat belt and said, "My granny has been baking cakes for you all week. Fairy cakes and profiteroles and chocolate eclairs ... they're my favourite... Do you like cakes, Tao?"

"I love cakes," I told her. "Kate makes these big lumpy cakes all covered in chocolate – they look terrible but they taste like heaven."

"That is so true," added Dad, turning around and smiling at me. "That's one thing I do miss ... Kate's cakes!"

I felt a bubble of happiness in my tummy when Dad said that. When he gets fed up with Jo and comes back to live with us, I'll tell Kate to make the biggest cake ever.

"Well, nobody likes cakes as much as my granny," said Mimi, her eyes wide like plates. "Actually, that's why she's so fat, at least that's what my grandad says when he's teasing her, which is all the time."

"Here we are," interrupted Paul, and he stopped the car in front of a red-brick house with a long front garden.

My hands felt sticky again and I wished that he'd just keep on driving and never stop.

Chapter 12

There was nobody in the house when Paul opened the door.

"I bet they're hiding," said Mimi. But then a girl's voice could be heard yelling from the back garden.

"We're out here! Come on, hurry up or you'll miss it. The egg is hatching!"

"The egg is hatching!" screamed Mimi. "Come on, Tao! Hurry up, we don't want to miss this!" She grabbed my hand and we ran through the house and out the back door, which was open, and into a big wooden shed where there were three people kneeling down around a very strong light bulb. They were all looking into a tray of straw with six brown eggs in it.

There was the dog, Sparkler, as well, wagging her tail and rushing about all excited, but nobody was paying her any attention.

"Hi, Tao," said a girl who was obviously Sally because she was all in black. "You look like Mimi." She said that without even looking up at me, so I don't know how she knew. "You're just in time to see my first chick hatching."

"Hi, Sally," I mumbled. "Hi, Conor." I knew him from his photo.

"Hi, Tao," said Conor. "Kneel down here and you'll be able to see." He shuffled over a bit to make room for me, and Mimi squashed herself in beside.

"Hi, George," said Mimi to the other boy who was there. He had long hair with what looked like ketchup in it, and a lot of spots. "This is my twin brother, Tao," she added, introducing me.

"Peace, man," said George and made peace signs to me with both hands. "I dig your timing, man. Just as the first egg is about to blow. Cool."

He was right. One of the eggs, which looked like just an ordinary brown hen's egg and had been rocking gently back and forth, cracked down the middle and a tiny chick all covered in sticky spittle tumbled out.

"Aw!" said Mimi.

"Yes!" shouted Sally.

"Man!" said George.

Conor and I just stared at the little chick stumbling about in its glass box.

"You know what this means?" said Sally. "Organic eggs!"

"Sounds good to me, young lady," said my dad, who had just come into the shed behind Paul. "You must be Sally?" he added, holding out his hand to her.

Then he shook Conor's hand and then George's.

"So where's the mother hen then?" he asked Sally, which was a good question.

"In Scotland," blurted out Mimi.

Sally gave her a look.

"I bought the eggs on the Internet," Sally explained. "I bought six, but they probably won't all hatch. The average is about three."

"But they did come from Scotland," insisted Mimi.

"Och, aye," said Conor. "It's a wee chick from Glasgow."

Everyone laughed at that and Sally picked up the tiny chick in her hands. It was very cute.

"What are you going to call it, hon?" Paul asked her, petting it with his finger.

"Cluck?" suggested George.

"I'm not calling it Cluck!" said Sally.

"Nessie? After the monster," said Conor. "Seeing as

it's from Scotland… Or Braveheart."

"Don't be so stupid, Conor," snapped Sally. "It's much too small to be called after some makey-up monster."

"The Loch Ness monster is not makey-up!" Mimi interrupted crossly. "I saw a photo of it in a book. It's a real monster … ask anyone!"

"Don't be so stupid, Mimi," said Sally sharply, and Mimi went red and stuck out her tongue when Sally wasn't looking.

"Scottie?" I said quietly. It just popped out. Sally looked at me … she was a very scary person.

"That's good," she said. "Scottie," she repeated, talking to the chick in her hand. "Little Scottie it is then. Thanks, Tao."

"Cool," said George.

I know that it's a bit silly, but I felt quite proud of myself.

Dad winked at me. Then Paul told Sally to put Scottie back into the incubator thing, because it was time to go and eat and the visitors must be starving.

Dinner was in the dining room and not in the kitchen, "Which it usually is," explained Mimi, "except when we have important visitors like you and your dad."

Paul barbecued steaks outside the back door, which

tasted great, but Sally wouldn't touch hers because cows were destroying the planet.

"Give it a rest, Sally," moaned Conor. "Don't mind her, Tao. She's mad in the head!"

Mimi nodded at me across the table as if to say "yes, she is". If Sally wasn't so fierce, I would have laughed.

"No, she's right, man," said George, his mouth full of meat. "Cows fart all day, man. It's bad news. All that gas heating up the planet."

Mimi spluttered when he said that and the water she was drinking squirted out of her nose and mouth. Conor put his hand under his arm and made a rude noise.

"Enough, George! Conor, behave yourself!" said Paul crossly. "We've got guests!"

"Sorry, man," mumbled George. "But straight up, man, nobody should be eating beef."

"You're eating beef, George," I said quietly. I was beginning to feel a bit braver.

George was silent then. Steadily chewing with his mouth open. Everybody was looking at him, but that didn't seem to worry him. He just nodded and said, "Fair point, man. Fair point."

Then he put another forkful of meat into his mouth. Mimi raised her eyes to heaven and I couldn't keep the laugh that was inside me inside me any longer. It just burst out and everybody laughed, even George. Except Sally, who looked very grumpy as she moved a lettuce leaf around her plate.

Then everybody started asking me lots of questions … about everything. After dinner, Mimi's grandparents arrived (were they my grandparents now, as well?) and there were more questions, especially from the granny. Mimi's cousins, Emmet and Emma, and their mum, Aunt B (which is short for Betty), arrived too and I was quizzed all over again.

It was a good day, but I was glad when Paul drove us to our hotel and we could be on our own again at last. It had been a long day as well and I was tired out. All I wanted to do was go to bed. We found our room and I kicked off my shoes and crawled into the bed nearest the door. I don't even remember saying goodnight to Dad.

Chapter 13

The breakfast in the hotel was huge. It was a full Irish breakfast, which is basically a big fry-up.

"Lovely now and again," said Dad, "but I wouldn't recommend tucking into that calorie fest every day! I'll have to do an extra round of golf to burn that lot off."

Dad was leaving to go to the airport by taxi at eleven and Mimi and her dad were coming to collect me at any time now.

"You will be all right on your own without me?" asked Dad.

"Yes. Of course I will," I answered more bravely than I felt.

I wondered what he would have done if I had said no.

"Well, you won't be lonely, that's for sure," he laughed, zipping his bag closed. "Mimi is a great kid, isn't she?"

"She's nice," I said.

"She's more than nice, Tao! She's full of beans."

I was feeling a bit shy now that I would be all on my own with all these people who seemed to all be full of beans!

"They gave you quite a grilling yesterday, didn't they?" continued Dad. He was sitting on one bed and I was sitting on the other. "It was the third degree. Especially the granny!"

He was right. Mimi's granny had wanted to know everything.

"What is your favourite food, Tao?"

"When did your parents get separated, Tao?"

"How far away does your dad live, Tao?"

"How old are his twins, Tao?"

"How old is Jo, Tao?"

"Is she married to your dad, Tao?"

"How do you feel about finding out you have a twin sister after all these years, Tao?"

"Does Kate work in the vegetable shop every day, Tao?"

"What do you want to be when you grow up, Tao?"

"Who is your best friend, Tao?"

On and on until Mimi's grandad stopped her. "Leave the boy alone, woman!" he told her. "You're worse than the CIA!"

"Curiosity killed the cat," chipped in Mimi.

"And too many cakes made her fat!" added the grandad with a big laugh. Granny pursed her lips when he said that.

"Don't mind that old fool," said Granny and was about to start firing more questions at me, but Mimi dragged me away to meet her cousin Emma.

"Who was, what's his name – the hippy chap?" asked Dad.

"George?"

"Yes. That guy. Is he Sally's boyfriend? Because if he is, he's a brave boy!" laughed Dad. "She's a fierce young lady. I wouldn't step on her toes, Tao."

I had no intention of stepping on Sally's toes. Adults say the most stupid things sometimes.

"She cornered you too, didn't she?" he added.

"She wanted to know all about The Happy Pear," I told him. "She wanted to know did it sell organic vegetables and whether we bought our fruit and veg locally and did Kate grow any vegetables herself and then she gave me a lecture about the carbon footprint of food that comes from faraway lands. I didn't understand half of what she said."

Dad laughed.

"Well, she should get on well with your mother!" he said. "They're both fanatics."

I felt a bit fed up when he said that. I wished he could for once say something about Kate that didn't sound just a bit nasty. Then he got a call from the desk to say that Paul and Mimi had arrived and so had his taxi.

"You be good, Tao," said Dad as he hugged me before getting into the taxi. "And don't let this little minx lead you into mischief!" he teased, tweaking Mimi's nose.

"Don't worry, we'll look after him," called out Paul as the taxi pulled away. Mimi took my hand and we both waved. I was glad that Kalem and David weren't there to see me holding a girl's hand.

Chapter 14

For the next two days before Kate came, I slept in Conor's room on a mattress on the floor. He said he would sleep on the mattress and I could take the bed, but I said that I would prefer the mattress. Mimi came in in her nightie and gave me a big hug goodnight. "And don't let the bugs bite!" she called cheerfully. Then she stuck out her tongue at Conor and ran off to her room laughing.

"If Mimi is your sister and I am her brother and you are her brother," said Conor from his bed, "then what are we to each other, Tao?"

It was very dark in the room. We couldn't see each other and that somehow made it easier to talk. I had been a bit worried about Conor. He seemed very friendly, but he was already a teenager with spots and I was afraid he might not be bothered with me.

"Brothers, I suppose," I said.

"But you support Wolves and I support Man U," he said in a serious voice, "which is bad news. No brother of mine can support Wolves. Sorry."

"What's wrong with Wolves?" I asked. I hoped that he was only messing.

"They're rubbish," he said. "But it's not too late to change, Tao. You could support a good team like Man U. What do you think? Then I'd let you be my brother."

I thought about my answer to that for a moment.

"You are obviously considering it," said Conor.

"Well. No," I had to tell him. "Some things are more important than brothers. Like supporting your football team, no matter what."

It was Conor's turn to be quiet now.

"You're right, Tao" he said at last. "No brother of mine would change football teams just like that. You've passed the test. I'll let you be my brother. Shake."

My eyes were growing used to the darkness and I could see Conor's hand reaching out. I shook it. It was a strong man's handshake.

"I didn't know that it was a test," I said.

"It wasn't really," answered Conor. "I just made that up. Goodnight, bro."

* * *

Earlier in the day, Conor and Sally had had a big fight because Conor wanted to practise his drums in the shed and Sally would not allow him because Scottie would be traumatized. I was watching telly with Mimi, but it was really wild. Sally was screaming that Conor was selfish and self-centred and didn't give a damn about bursting the eardrums of a poor chick barely one day old and Conor was shouting back that his drums weren't half as bad as her screaming ... but his voice was doing this weird thing – it was changing from really low to really high.

"His voice is breaking," explained Mimi. "It happens to boys. It will happen to you too, Tao."

I didn't like the sound of that.

"Can it be fixed?" I asked.

Mimi thought for a moment. She didn't seem too sure.

"We'll ask Orla when she comes. She knows everything."

So now we were watching "Southsiders", the worst soap ever, and listening to Conor and Sally having World War III. Not that Mimi seemed to notice, even though the house shook when Sally slammed her bedroom door.

"Sally gets very cross, doesn't she?" I said.

"It's just hermoans going crazy," answered Mimi, her eyes glued to the telly. She really seemed to like this programme. Girls are very strange.

"Her what?"

"Hermoans. Aunty B told me all about it. It happens to all girls when they become teenagers."

"Oh," I said. I was very confused.

"It'll happen to me too." Mimi shrugged. "I will shout at everyone and go mad and cry and put rings in my nose and slam doors and wear black and be moody and rude to everyone... Just like Sally. My moans will be all over the place."

"How come Conor isn't like that?" I said. "He is a teenager."

"It doesn't happen to boys," explained Mimi. "That's why they are called hermoans and not his-moans."

"It all sounds a bit mad to me," I said.

"Oh, don't worry about it!" laughed Mimi. "It's just a girl thing."

Then the doorbell rang and it was Mimi's friend Orla, who said that she had come to give me the "once-over" ... whatever that meant. Right behind her, coming up the driveway, were Mimi's cousins, Emma and Emmett. Emmett had come to practise with Conor's rock group.

* * *

It was strange spending all afternoon with girls. Kalem and David would have teased me about it, but it was fun. Orla and Emma gave me and Mimi a twin test. They asked questions that we had to answer straight away and together.

Orla: Favourite colour?

Mimi and Tao: Red.

Emma: Lucky number?

Mimi and Tao: Ten.

Orla: Star sign?

Mimi and Tao: Pisces (of course ... duh! ... we are twins!)

Emma: Favourite food?

Mimi and Tao: Chocolate.

"Uncanny," said Orla. "You really are twins!"

Then she told one of her jokes.

"Did you hear about the Mexican woman who had twin boys?"

"I'm not going to get this joke, am I?" said Mimi.

"No, probably not," said Orla.

"What's the answer?" said Emma, impatiently.

"She called one Hose A and the other Hose B."

There was silence for a moment. Mimi wasn't the only one who didn't get it. Then Emma said, "I think

I get it, Orla," and then she laughed. But it sounded a bit forced. Then she added, "No … maybe I don't…"

Orla sighed and shook her head.

"Let's see how Scottie is coping with the racket," she said and Mimi led the way out to the shed.

Later that night as we lay in our beds, Conor asked, "So what did you think of our rock group, Tao?" I was glad it was dark and he couldn't see my face.

"You're loud," I said, which I don't think was what he wanted to hear. He went quiet for a moment.

"The chicks liked us," he said and laughed. "Sally was wrong about that."

In fact, two more eggs had hatched while they were playing.

"The chicks always love rock 'n' roll," George had said. He wanted to call them the Rock Chicks but Sally wouldn't allow it.

"They are not pets," she said. "They are working animals who will have to earn their keep. So no names, except for Scottie, and that's final."

Aunty B, who had arrived to collect Emma and Emmet, agreed with her. "You don't name farm animals," she said. "You don't want to know a chicken's name when one day you will have to wring that chicken's neck."

"Aw, Mum!" said Emma. "No one is going to wring the Rock Chicks' necks! Are they, Sally?"

Sally didn't answer that. She just hammered another long nail into the chicken house she was building with George.

"It might not be a thing of beauty, man," said George, stepping back to admire their work, "but it's … cool!"

"What do you think of Sally's chicken coop, Tao?" asked Conor from his bed.

"Well, it is solid," I answered, because I couldn't think of anything else good to say about it.

"It's solid, all right," said Conor. "Big and ugly but definitely solid! Goodnight."

"Goodnight," I answered sleepily. It had been another good day but now all I wanted to do was sleep. Tomorrow evening Kate would be here. I wondered what she'd make of this big noisy family.

Chapter 15

We met Kate off the airport bus. The bus stop was in the middle of the main street and there were a lot of people around but Kate didn't care.

"Tao!" she called out as soon as she stepped off the bus. She dropped both her bags and wrapped me up in one of her special hugs. "ImissedyouImissedyou-Imissedyou," she said over and over, putting kisses all over my face. I wished she'd stop.

"It's only been three days," I tried to say.

Then Kate saw Mimi and I could see what was going to happen.

"Mimi!" she said, and her arms opened and now it was Mimi's turn to be hugged to death. "Iloveyoualready. IdoIdoIdo!"

I wondered what Mimi would make of my mad mother, but she seemed quite happy. Paul just stood there with a big smile on his face. Even his eyes seemed to be grinning. Everyone who passed by glanced at us and smiled. It would have been so embarrassing at home, but nobody knew me here so I didn't mind so much.

"Paul!" said Kate, releasing Mimi at last.

"Your mum is funny," Mimi whispered in my ear while Kate gave Paul a big hug too, but not quite such a big squeeze. At least I hoped not.

"She's also completely insane," I whispered back to Mimi and she giggled.

Back at the house, Conor and Sally got hugs too. Conor kept his hands by his sides and went all red, but Sally gave a big hug back, which wasn't what I expected.

"I want to see these chicks that I've been hearing all about," said Kate, gently pushing Sally towards the back door as if she knew the way, and Sally was laughing!

So we were all out in the shed, but not before Kate had met Sparkler and practically hugged her too and now the dog was jumping all over Kate and Paul had to pull her off and lock her in the house.

The three chicks were in a box of sawdust under

the heat lamp and Sally was explaining all about them to Kate and how they had to be kept at 35 degrees of heat until they were bigger and could go in the hen house.

I wasn't sure which chick was which anymore, but Mimi pointed at one of them and said that that was Scottie and that I had named him, and Kate smiled at me and squeezed my shoulder and asked could she pick the chick up.

"Of course," said Sally, even though she had not let anyone touch the chicks before!

Of course, Kate got all soppy when she was holding the chick.

"Aw!" she crooned as the tiny chick cheeped. "Chicks are so much cuter than rats." And she winked at me.

"You mean mice," I corrected her.

"You take him," she said and she passed the chick to Mimi, who glanced across at Sally first, then held the warm little bundle to her face. Sally picked up another one and passed it to me. You could feel its bones underneath the fluff. It was weird. Nearly as weird as Sally being friendly.

Even though it was getting a bit late, Paul said that Mimi and I should take Sparkler for a walk because he and Kate had lots of boring adult things to discuss. I wondered what they were. At home, I would have stayed outside the door and eavesdropped.

"I bet they are talking about us," said Mimi as soon as we were outside the gate. "Do you ever listen outside the door when adults chat, Tao?" she asked me.

"No, of course not," I said. "Do you?"

Mimi didn't answer straight away. I must have grinned when she said, "No, I don't either. Of course not," because she smiled and added, "Well ... sometimes."

"Me too," I laughed.

Sparkler was one of those silly dogs who pulls at the lead and sniffs at everything and wraps the lead around poles and trees, so we weren't getting very far. Then she did a poo!

"Ah, no! I hate that!" said Mimi, and she pulled a plastic bag out of her pocket. "You hold the dog," she said and handed me the lead.

She put the bag on her hand and, with her nose all wrinkled up, she picked up the poo and tied it into the bag. She held the smelly bag by the tips of her fingers.

"That is gross," I said, and held my nose.

"I hate dog's bottoms," she said. "They should stick a cork in them!"

Luckily there was a dog-poo bin on the next pole so she could get rid of the stinky bag.

"This bully called Sarah used to call me Stinky Chinky at school," said Mimi, "after my mammy died."

She was quiet then.

"Were people not nice to you when your mammy died?" I asked her.

"Yeah, they were," Mimi said, "except for Sarah. Everyone gave me hugs and sweets and things. Miss Lemon, who owns the shop, used to give me free sweets every day. She still does sometimes."

"We should go there," I said, but Mimi just smiled. She was thinking of something else.

Sparkler had stopped to check out another amazing smell, so we had stopped too.

"They kept saying how sad it was for me to lose my mother," said Mimi, "but I didn't lose her ... she was run over by a bus. Adults say really stupid things sometimes. And they were always talking about me like I wasn't there," continued Mimi, "saying things like 'the poor child, to have her mother taken away so young' like she was grabbed out of my hands or something!"

"Were you very sad?" I asked her. "I would be."

"Yes," said Mimi, and I could see that she was sad just thinking about it. "Everyone said that Dad was 'beside himself with grief'. What's that supposed to mean, anyway?"

I shrugged. I didn't know what it was supposed to mean. We turned and started walking home.

"He used to cook us burnt pizza every day for months afterwards, but it got better after a bit," said Mimi and then she added, "I like your mum. She is not like your dad, is she?"

"How do you mean?" I asked her. I sort of knew what she meant, but I was surprised when she said it.

"You know," she said, "the way he's all smart and serious and Kate is … well, she's a bit mad, isn't she? In a nice way. It's hard to imagine them being married."

"Well, they were," I said a bit sharply, "until Jo came along. She wrecked everything."

"Do you hate her?" asked Mimi.

"Yes," I said. "I do."

"Then I hate her too," said Mimi.

"But you haven't even met her!" I said. "You might like her. She's quite nice, you know."

Mimi laughed when I said that.

"Make up your mind!" she said.

Even though I was a bit cross with all this talk about Jo, I had to smile because what I had said sounded stupid even to me.

But I didn't want to talk about it anymore, so I

asked Mimi did the girl still call her Stinky Chinky?

"Sarah?" answered Mimi. "No, I said I'd punch her lights out if she didn't stop bullying me. She's sort of a friend now."

We were nearly home and it was getting dark. I smiled at the thought of Mimi beating anybody up. But I didn't say anything.

That night before I fell asleep, Conor said, "Your mum is like our rock group ... loud!"

He didn't say it in a bad way, but I said, "She's not always like that."

"She's probably a bit nervous meeting all of us," said Conor.

I hadn't thought about it like that. I had thought that I would be the only one nervous about meeting Mimi and her family.

"Don't get me wrong," continued Conor. "I think she's cool ... as George would say."

I had never thought of Kate as being cool either. Still, if Conor thought she was, then ... maybe she was!

"So, this mouse of yours..." Conor started saying.

"Rodent?" I asked, as if I had more than one.

"Yeah," said Conor. "Who is looking after him?"

"Jo," I told him, even though I didn't like mentioning her name.

"Your dad's girlfriend?"

"S'pose so," I muttered, but there must have been something in the way I said it because Conor was quiet for a bit and then he said, "Would you like your dad to come back and live with you and Kate?"

"Yes, I would," I said and for no reason my eyes suddenly started to water. I was glad it was dark.

Conor didn't say anything else for a long time after that. Neither did I.

"'Night, Tao," he said at last.

"'Night, Conor," I said, but I lay awake looking into the dark for a long time before I eventually drifted off.

Chapter 16

On Easter Sunday, Mimi's grandparents held a big party in their house for all the family.

"It's in your honour, Tao," said Grandad when we arrived, which was a bit scary.

I had met most of Mimi's uncles and aunts and cousins already, but Kate had to be introduced to them all so there was another big round of hugs.

Aunt M (whose real name is Marigold) arrived with her husband Nicholas. No one called him Uncle Nicholas. Maybe he was too young. She was pregnant, but she still arrived on the back of Nicholas's motorbike and Granny flew into a rage about that.

"That is the most irresponsible thing that I have

ever heard of," she told Aunt M, who completely ignored her and walked straight over to Kate and gave her a big hug.

"You'll find that we're not all as hysterical as my mother," she said to Kate. Granny looked fit to burst. Nicholas just stood there looking at the floor.

"Hi, Tao," Aunt M said to me and ruffled my hair. "Are you surviving in that mad house?"

"Hi, Aunt M," I said shyly. Aunt M is a very pretty lady and I never know what to say to her.

"Aunt M and Granny don't always get on," Mimi whispered to me. Then she asked me did I want to feel the baby move in Aunt M's tummy? I didn't know what to say when Mimi said that. I think I went bright red, but Mimi didn't seem to notice.

"Tao wants to feel your tummy," she told her aunt and she put her two hands right on the middle of Aunt M's big round belly.

"No…" I started to say, but I was too late.

"Of course you can," said Aunt M and took my hand and placed it on her tummy. I was like Nicholas, staring at the floor. Then something moved under my hand. It was weird – it was like an alien under her skin.

"Did you feel that, Tao?" asked Aunt M. She had a kind voice. I nodded. "That was the baby kicking."

"Weird," I mumbled and everyone laughed.

I'm not sure that I liked the feeling but I smiled and she let go of my hand.

The last guests to arrive were Uncle Boris and Aunt L (short for Lupin – all the aunts except Betty are called after flowers) and a toddler called Wee Billy. He was about the same age as Rachel and Roger and just as mad. They had driven down from Belfast.

"How's my wee lass?" roared Uncle Boris and swung Mimi into the air.

"And this must be the wee laddie?" he roared at me and putting down Mimi, he grabbed me under the arms and lifted me right up and swung me around. He was a very big man.

"Don't even try it!" laughed Kate when he put me down and turned to her. Uncle Boris hesitated a moment then looked around the room. His eyes were twinkling … then he grabbed Kate in a big bear hug and lifted her off the floor! Everyone laughed then.

"Imagine having to live with that man!" said Aunt L as she shook my hand and then hugged Kate.

The best part of the day was the egg hunt. All the adults sat on the patio and drank wine while the children searched the garden for eggs. Kate sat beside Paul and every few minutes I could hear her big laugh.

"She hasn't snorted yet," said Mimi, who had decided to help me look for eggs because she was a champion egg-hunter ... or so she said.

"She will. Just wait," I said. I hadn't found any eggs yet, but Mimi kept spotting them in the most hidden away places.

"You missed that one," she said as she pulled a little egg out of the frame of the garden bench, where I had just looked.

Sally was helping Wee Billy, who was haring around the garden like a wild man, screaming his head off.

"Oh, please don't give him any more chocolate," moaned Aunt L. "He's as high as a kite."

Conor and Emmett were wandering around with a bag for eggs as well, but they were chatting away and weren't really looking.

Emma was trying to find more than Mimi and kept shouting at her every time she found an egg.

"Have you found any yet, Dig? You blind old fool!" she yelled.

"More than you, Dag!" Mimi shouted back. "We call each other Dig and Dag," she explained to me as she picked another little egg that I had completely missed out of a daffodil.

"Too much chocolate will give you windy bottoms,

Dig," shouted Emma from the top of the garden. "You know how you are!"

The adults on the patio laughed when they heard that.

"That is so true," said Aunt M, popping a chocolate sweet into her mouth.

"Go easy there, Marigold," said Granny. "That baby fat is hard to shift."

Aunt M gave her mother a look and popped another sweet into her mouth. "Well, you'd know all about that, Mother, wouldn't you?"

"Wooooh!" said everyone together and Kate let out a big snorting laugh.

"Yes!" said Mimi loudly. "She really does snort!"

Well, that really set Kate off and soon everyone was laughing their heads off.

I was sorry when the day was over and we had to go home.

Conor spent the night with his cousin Emmett, so I was alone in his room. I was half asleep when the door quietly opened and Mimi tiptoed in. She sat down on the end of my mattress.

"I can't sleep," she said. "I had too much chocolate. It makes me hyper." Then she started giggling and farted. "It makes me do windy bottoms, too," she laughed.

"That's not good for the planet," I said.

"My daddy likes your mum," she said then.

I was quiet when she said that.

"They're still downstairs talking away," continued Mimi. "You can hear them in my room if you put your ear on the floor."

"What are they saying?" I asked.

"I don't know," said Mimi. "They are talking too quietly."

Well, that wasn't much use.

"How do you know that they like each other then?" I asked her.

"Oh, you know…" said Mimi. "Girls just know these things."

Mimi went back to her own bed soon after that but I lay awake for a long time, just thinking. I wished that Kate and I weren't going home tomorrow.

Chapter 17

On the plane home, Kate asked me lots of questions.

"Weren't they a lovely family, Tao?"

"Yes."

"Isn't Mimi a pet, Tao?"

"Yes."

"Nice house haven't they, Tao?"

"Yes."

"Sally might be all prickly on the outside, but underneath she's a marshmallow, would you agree, Tao?"

"No."

"As for Conor – you really hit it off with him, didn't you, Tao?"

"Yes."

"Mimi's grandmother thinks you're a dote, Tao."

"She thinks I'm a what?"

"A dote," said Kate. "It means you're a pet."

"Oh ... that's OK then."

"Paul isn't a bit like your dad is he, Tao?"

"How do you mean?" I asked suspiciously.

"Well," said Kate slowly, and I could see that she was choosing her words carefully. "He's ... different, that's all."

I knew that wasn't all but I didn't want Kate to say any more.

"I s'pose so," I said and I pretended to read the comic I had bought in the airport.

Kate sighed and opened her book. The plane landed soon after.

Jo dropped Rodent back that evening. It was the first time she had ever come to our house. Kate was first to the door, but I was right behind her in the hall.

"Oh, hello," said Kate, surprised. Even from behind I could see her stiffen. "Tao," she called. "It's for you."

"I've brought back your mouse," Jo said to me. She had to put her head to one side to see around Kate.

"Excuse me," said Kate, and she turned on her heel and walked straight past me into the kitchen and closed the door behind her. Her lips were thin and her face was white.

"Did you have a nice time in Ireland?" asked Jo, as she handed me the cage. Her face was red. I couldn't understand why Dad hadn't come himself.

"Why didn't my dad bring Rodent back?" I asked her.

"He was busy," she said. "Anyway, Rodent is back home now and might I say he was a very popular guest in our house... Weren't you, Rodent?" she said to Rodent who was peeping his head out of the straw.

"Bye now," she said in a cheery voice that sounded put on. "See you on Saturday and you can tell me all about your holiday." Then, as she turned to go, she stopped and said, "Oh, I nearly forgot. We got Rodent a little toy." She handed me a plastic bag with some sort of ball in it. "The twins loved watching him play in this."

"Thanks," I mumbled and she was gone.

I put the cage back up in my room before going down to Kate. Rodent was glad to see me and came straight into my hand when I opened the cage door.

"Hi, Rodent," I said, "welcome home," and I petted his back. His coat looked nice and shiny. I could see that he had been well looked after, but he was obviously happy to be home. At least I think he was because he kept twitching his nose. The ball in the bag was one of those clear plastic ones that you put a mouse in and they can run around the floor and not escape. I thought that I would try it out later on.

Downstairs, Kate was sitting at the table, sipping a mug of her herbal tea. She still looked very pale.

"Sorry about that," she said when I came in, but I didn't know what she was sorry about. "It's just that when I opened the door and there was the rat … I mean mouse. And Jo. I felt a bit faint."

"Are you all right now?" I asked her a bit crossly. She didn't have to explain everything.

"I hope Jo didn't think I was rude?" she said.

"I hope she did," I said and went out into the garden to practise my keepie-uppies.

It was Dad's fault for not bringing Rodent home himself.

The next day, I was at David's house with Kalem playing Wii games. They had questions too.

"So what was Mimi like then?" asked Kalem.

"What he really wants to know is what was Emma like," teased David.

David and I were playing boxing and it was hard to concentrate and answer questions. The best way to win Wii boxing is to throw punches as fast as you

can and not bother about defence. We were both boxing like madmen and moving closer and closer to the
telly. In a minute one of us was going to end up boxing the box!

After three rounds, we were both exhausted and
collapsed on the couch.

"Loser!" said David.

"I'll beat you at golf," I told him.

"I'll beat you at tennis," he answered.

"I'll beat you at basketball," I said.

"I'll beat you at…"

"Oh, shut up you two!" shouted Kalem, who never
plays Wii, "and tell us about your trip and Mimi and
all that stuff."

"Is she taller than you?" David wanted to know.

"No, she's the same height," I told him. "Well, I'm
probably a bit taller."

"Yeah, sure you are," jeered Kalem.

"What about the vampire?" David asked. "Are they
bite marks I see on your neck?" And he tried to pull
down the collar of my shirt to look.

"Get off," I cried and pushed him away. "Anyway,
Mimi is coming over with her dad in June, so you can
find out everything for yourself."

"Is the vampire coming?" asked David. "We'll have
to get garlic."

"Sally's a vegetarian," I said, "so there goes your vampire theory."

"That's just her disguise," said David, making big boggly eyes. "A vegetarian by day ... a blood-sucking vampire by night!"

Kalem sighed and shook his head slowly.

"David," he said.

"What?" said David.

"You're an idiot."

Chapter 18

Paul had decided to bring Mimi over to visit me for the long weekend in June. Conor couldn't come because he had to study for his tests and Sally had to stay in Ireland to look after her garden and her hens, which Mimi said were turning out to be more trouble than they were worth. Their granny and grandad would move into their house to look after them while Mimi and Paul were with us. Mimi said that she was glad she wasn't staying at home because it was going to be fireworks between her granny and Sally because her granny thought that being a vegetarian was codswallop and young bones needed meat.

"Sounds like war!" said Kate.

I think that Kate was more excited than I was about Paul and Mimi coming over. Every evening she was on the phone to Paul and they would chat for hours.

"I think your mother has taken a shine to this Paul chap," said Willy with a grin, when I dropped into The Happy Pear on the way home from school.

"Stop that, you!" laughed Kate and waggled her finger at him, but I didn't see what was so funny.

"Kate," Willy said, looking through a book of wise sayings that a customer had given him. "What about this one for over the small window – *Happiness is the china shop. Love is the bull.* It's by some chap called Mencken."

"I think I'll put *you* over the small window if you don't stop your nonsense," she said, but you could tell she was enjoying being teased. Since Easter, she had been like this. Silly and embarrassing. I just hoped she behaved herself when Mimi and Paul came.

The week before they arrived was very busy. The whole house had to get a going-over, apparently. Kate had never bothered much with housework before, but now she was like a madwoman. Dusting and hoovering and painting and washing stuff and humming all the time.

"You do know that Mimi is actually coming to see

me?" I said to her one day.

"Of course, love," she said and grabbed me for a quick hug and kisses. "That's why the place has to look its best."

"Your mum is a serial kisser," Kalem once told me.

"Do you mean like a serial killer?" asked David with wide eyes.

"Yes," I agreed gloomily, "only worse." And they both laughed.

Jo was very curious to meet "the great Mimi in person" as she kept saying, even though Mimi had nothing to do with her. Rachel and Roger had gone completely off their heads with excitement. Charging around shouting, "MIMIMIMIMIMIMIMIMIMIMIMIMIMIMIMIMIMI" was now their favourite game.

The Head Honcho wanted to know was she any good at football because he was looking for a new centre-half to replace the very distracted one he now had! Of course, he meant me.

Dad was the only calm one.

"Mimi will be the nervous one," he said. "It's an away game for her this time, but it will all be fine, you'll see."

I wished I was as sure as he was. What if Mimi didn't like my house or my friends? What if we didn't know what to say to each other? What if Kate drove her mad with her hugs?

But Dad just laughed and tousled my hair and called me an old worry-head.

Chapter 19

The best thing we did when Paul and Mimi were with us was the land yachts. Kate heard about it from one of the customers and although it was quite a long drive to the beach, it was worth it. Kalem came as well. David had to go to visit someone, which was just as well because there wasn't room in the car for him.

On the way, Kalem told Mimi all about his latest great invention.

"Square sausages!" he declared. "What do you think?"

"Of what?" she said and looked very puzzled.

"Square sausages are the answer to the age-old problem of the rolling sausage," said Kalem.

"The rolling sausage?" I interrupted. I hadn't a clue what he was talking about.

"You know the way when you fry sausages in the pan and you try to turn them to cook all the sides evenly all over and they keep rolling back..."

"Yeah, they do roll!" said Mimi, suddenly excited.

"Well," said Kalem, "square sausages wouldn't roll."

"No, they wouldn't!" said Mimi, and looked at Kalem like he was some kind of genius.

"Don't encourage him, Mimi," I said. "If his head gets any bigger it will burst."

Kalem just looked smug.

The beach was miles long. I couldn't even see the end of it and the sand was hard. The sea was grey. At the top of the beach was a hut surrounded by yachts on wheels – the ones that sail along the sand.

Soon we were all sitting in the land yachts with helmets on our heads and the man who rented them out was shouting instructions at us.

"Keep the sail tight by pulling the left-hand rope and when you reach those yellow cones pull the right rope and let the left go slack. That will turn the yacht. Are you listening to me, young one?" he shouted at Mimi, who was staring straight ahead and blowing out her cheeks. She nodded but I don't think she had listened to a word.

"Right!" shouted Paul, who looked much too big for his yacht. "An ice cream for anyone who beats me!"

"Racing is not permitted," said the man.

"Oh," said Paul. "Sorry about that. No racing, you lot – you heard the man."

But as soon as the man had turned his back and walked a bit away, Paul looked down the line of us in our yachts and mouthed the words, "Race on!"

It was brilliant and scary at the same time. As soon as we raised our sails, the wind caught them and we were off, speeding down the empty beach. Kate and Paul crashed into each other straight away and had to start again. Kalem got off to a flying start. I got off to a slower start, but there was no way he was going to beat me. Mimi was nowhere to be seen, so she must have been behind us.

"Eat your hearts out, losers!" Kalem jeered, but he made a mess of turning around the cone. "Which stupid rope am I supposed to pull?" he shouted as his yacht slowed right down.

My yacht nearly went over as I skidded around the cone on two wheels. I was neck and neck with Kalem now and pulling the rope as hard as I could.

"Hi, Tao," shouted Paul as he passed me going the other way. Kate was still stuck at the starting line and the man was giving her a push. There was no sign of Mimi, but I wasn't going to turn my head to look.

"Watch the master in action," I shouted across to Kalem. Our wheels were nearly touching. It was like the chariot race in *Ben-Hur*.

But he was heavier than me and the sand was a bit softer here.

"See you later, alligator!" I yelled as I pulled past him and crossed the finish line. I loosened the sail and jumped up in the air.

"Well done, Tao!" called out Kalem, who is a much better loser than David.

But the man who owned the yachts was not happy.

"I said that racing was not permitted," he said. "There could have been a nasty accident with inexperienced drivers like yourselves on board."

"Sorry," we mumbled, but we weren't.

"As for that girl – she ignored all of my instructions," continued the man crossly, pointing at a land yacht way in the distance. "Will you look at her, halfway down the beach!"

"Oh, for God's sake," said Paul, who had just finished.

Mimi was nearly out of sight. She had obviously

forgotten to turn, or forgotten how to turn at the cones, and carried straight on … and on.

"I'll get her!" I shouted and jumped back into my yacht. I pulled up the sail and zoomed off after Mimi.

"That's your twin sister all over," Paul called after me, "never quite gets it right!" And he laughed.

She really was far away and there was no way I was going to catch her before the end of the beach. She looked tiny on her land yacht, her long black hair blowing out from under her blue helmet. But then she must have hit some soft sand because her yacht slowed right down and then it fell over sideways and Mimi fell out.

But in a second she was on her feet, jumping up and down and waving her arms around and yelling. The wind was blowing her voice away, but as I got nearer I could catch what she was shouting.

"I won! I won! I won!"

It was a long time before we got back to the top of the beach. And it had started to rain. Paul put his coat over Kate's head and Kalem was helping the man push the yachts into a shed.

"Did you not hear me say 'turn at the yellow cones', young lady?" the man said to Mimi as we climbed out of the yachts. "I have other customers waiting for these yachts." Which was hard to believe because, the beach was completely empty.

"What yellow cones?" asked a puzzled Mimi. The man just shook his head and everyone else laughed.

The next day, Dad came over to collect Mimi and me and take us back to his house. He came in to say hello to Paul, but with Kate standing there it felt uncomfortable and I was glad when Dad said, "Right Tao, Mimi, let's go – there are some very excited children in my house waiting to jump all over you."

He was only half right. Because when we got there, Rachel and Roger suddenly got all shy and hid behind Jo's legs, sucking their thumbs. I peeped around her legs and said to Roger, "This is Rachel!" and to Rachel I said, "And this is Roger!"

"NO!" shouted the twins and that was end of their shyness.

It was a noisy evening with a lot of running around the house and shouting and tickling but in the end the twins (Roger and Rachel, not me and Mimi) were tired out and we all sat down together on the couch to watch *Mary Poppins* while Dad and Jo made supper. I was the only one not sucking my thumb.

"She's a pet," Jo whispered to me before we left. I said nothing.

* * *

Before bedtime I put Rodent in the plastic running ball and Mimi and I crawled around the sitting room while Rodent ran this way and that … wherever the ball rolled. When it crashed into furniture he just darted off in a different direction.

"You're a looper, Rodent," said Mimi, when the ball crashed into her face (she was lying on her tummy on the floor). Rodent ignored her, of course, and raced off straight into the leg of the coffee table.

But after a while we forgot about him and watched telly, so neither of us noticed the ball opening and Rodent escaping.

When the programme was over I saw what had happened.

"Where's Rodent?" I asked, but, of course, Mimi didn't have a clue. We looked everywhere but he was nowhere to be found.

"He must have got out of the room," I said. The door was a little bit open.

"Don't worry, Tao," said Mimi. "We'll find him."

Well, I wasn't that worried but I was a little bit because he wasn't in the hall either.

Then we heard Paul in the kitchen.

"Easy does it. Make no sudden movements. And remember to breathe!"

Then we heard Kate giggling nervously.

Mimi put her finger to her lips and pushed open the kitchen door very gently. Through the crack we could see Kate's back. Paul was sitting in front of her. He saw us and winked but Kate didn't know we were there. She was sitting very still. Then I saw my mouse on her shoulder, sniffing her neck! I couldn't believe it. I pushed the door right open and Kate turned her head slowly and smiled at me.

"Rodent is on your neck!" I said.

"I know," said Kate, "and he tickles. Take him off me now please, Paul."

"You are brave," said Mimi to Kate, as Paul handed me back Rodent.

"Not as brave as Rodent," teased Paul and Kate gave him a little thump on the arm, but he just laughed.

"You can close your mouth now, Tao," said Kate and with her little finger she petted Rodent's head.

"But I thought…" I started to say.

"Yes, well," said Kate and put her arm around my shoulder and pulled me towards her for a half-hug. I was still holding Rodent. "As Paul says, if the mouse and I are going to have to live together, we'd better get used to each other."

"You've got to look your fears straight in the eyes," added Paul, "and then headbutt them!"

When she stopped laughing, Kate told us not to say that to Willy or it would be all over the walls of The Happy Pear. Then she shooed Mimi and I up to bed.

"Did you see that?" I said to Mimi as I put Rodent safely back in his cage.

"Yeah," said Mimi, "they were holding hands."

Which wasn't what I had meant.

"That was only to keep Kate calm," I said a bit sharply.

"Whatever," answered Mimi and she grinned, but I felt a bit fed up inside.

The next day at breakfast Mimi said, "I like Jo. She's very smiley, isn't she?"

"You said you hated her," I blurted out.

"That was before I met her," answered Mimi. "I think she's very nice."

Nobody said anything for a moment. I looked at Kate. She decided to smile.

"Yes," she said, "Jo is a good person."

I thought Mimi would be happy with that, but she looked at me and so did Paul.

"She's OK," I muttered into my cereal.

Everybody seemed to love Mimi. When I took her to Kalem's house, Angela said that she had all my good bits and none of my bad and then she dug her fingers into my sides and squeezed.

"And don't think I'm leaving you out, miss!" she shouted and dug her big hands into Mimi's sides.

"That's not such a good idea," Kalem warned his mother.

Mimi burst out laughing and let out one of her loud cracker-bums (which is one of her words for farts) and then she went all red.

"Oh nice one, Miss Mimi!" Angela laughed and held her nose with her fingers.

"Mimi, I'm going to honour you with one of my world-famous Willyisms … when I think of a good one," declared Willy when we dropped into The Happy Pear to say hello.

"Thank you," said Mimi politely, but she looked very confused. She looked at me and made one of her help-I-haven't-a-clue-what-anyone-is-talking-about faces. I could see Kate looking at her with a big silly smile on her face.

Even David thought that Mimi was OK … for a girl.

Just like at Easter, I was really sorry when it was time for Mimi to go home. On the last evening, Kate and Paul went for a long walk and Mimi and I watched telly for a while, but there was nothing good on.

"Let's play the Interview Game," suggested Mimi.

"I've never heard of that game," I told her, but she said it was easy.

Mimi said that she would be the interviewer first to show me how it goes. I sat on one chair and she sat on the other chair with our knees nearly touching.

"Right," said Mimi, "relax and forget about the TV cameras."

"I'll try," I said.

"Good afternoon, ladies and gentlemen," Mimi told her audience, "and welcome to 'The Saturday Interview'—"

"It's Tuesday," I corrected her.

"'The Tuesday Interview', then," she sighed, "and my very special guest today needs no introduction – it's Tao Clarke!"

She stopped for a moment then, to let the imaginary clapping and cheering die down. Then she turned to me with a big cheesy grin.

"Welcome to the show, Tao," she smiled.

I said, "Thank you."

"So, Tao Clarke, do you like marshmallows in hot chocolate?" was her first question.

That was easy peasy.

"Yes, I do."

"That was just to make you feel relaxed and at home," Mimi explained in a whisper. "All good interviewers do that. Then just when you think that it is going to be a doddle, they hit you with the hard question."

"I'm ready for it," I grinned. "Shoot!" Which is what Dad sometimes says.

"What age were you when your father left?" was her second question. Right out of the blue.

"I was seven," I said.

"Before that, did your parents fight all the time?" she asked like a shot.

"Yes," I answered too quickly. "I mean, no. I mean … what do you mean?" I was suddenly flustered.

Mimi had a mad gleam in her eye. "Did they fall out of love?" she asked, without giving me time to answer.

"I don't know," I said.

"Yes or no?" insisted Mimi. The audience was very quiet. Mimi was the interviewer from hell.

"Maybe … I don't know," I said. "It was all Jo's fault."

Mimi sat back, folded her arms and nodded her head wisely. "So do you blame Jo for breaking up your parents' marriage?" she asked slowly.

I was saved by the doorbell.

It was David and Kalem come to say goodbye to Mimi.

"Do you have Skype?" David asked her.

"No," said Mimi.

"Do you have MSN?"

"No," said Mimi.

"Do you have Facebook?"

"No," said Mimi.

"Oh," said David.

"You will just have to text her," said Kalem.

"Does Emma have Skype or MSN or Facebook?" said David. "Kalem wants to know."

"I do not!" said Kalem and thumped David on the arm, but he blushed all the same.

Then Kalem said "bye" and so did David, and Mimi gave them both hugs. They were both blushing when they left.

The car felt very empty when Kate and I drove back from the airport the next morning. Kate squeezed my knee and smiled but she seemed distracted.

"It won't be long, Tao honey," she said, "until the summer holidays. We'll see them again then."

I knew it wasn't long, but it seemed like ages.

That night, Mimi texted me.

> Nite nite bro. Tanks 4 d
> grt hols. Mimi XXX

And I texted back,

Nite nite sis
cya soon Tao XXX

Chapter 20

Kate was right. I didn't have long to wait until the summer holidays. Every evening she crossed off another day on the calendar.

"Only ten days to go…" she'd say in an excited voice.

"Only nine days to go… It's getting nearer, Tao!"

"Eight days, Tao… Oh, I can't wait!"

Seven … six … five … four … three … and every day she would get even more excited. It was very catching … and every day I got texts from Mimi saying how excited she was about the holiday.

> 2 days 2 go. I'm
> going 2 burst! Mimi XXX

Even Rachel and Roger were getting excited, and they weren't even coming.

"Tomorrowtomorrowtomorrowtomorrow," they shouted, charging around their kitchen.

"I'd love to be going on holiday," said Jo with a sigh. "You are so lucky, Tao."

I knew that I was lucky, but for some reason I didn't feel as excited as everyone else. I sighed.

She turned and looked at me. "What's up?" she asked, sitting down at the table. The twins had run out into the garden. But I wasn't going to tell her what was up, even if I knew what it was myself. Suddenly there was a lump in my throat.

"You do want to go on this holiday?" she asked, putting her hand on mine.

"Yes," I said, pulling my hand away. And I did want to.

She didn't say anything. She just kept looking at me. I felt like she was looking right into my head.

"Do you miss your dad sometimes?" she said in a very soft voice.

I wished she hadn't asked that, because now I could feel tears running silently down my face and I badly needed to blow my nose.

"Come here, you," she said. She stood up and came over to me. I thought she might try to hug me again, so I shook my head strongly to say no. She sighed and dropped her arms. Then she handed me a tissue. I dried my eyes and blew my nose loudly.

"OK now?" she asked.

"Yeah," I said. I felt very embarrassed. I was glad Dad hadn't been there to see me.

"And don't worry about Rodent," she smiled. "I will treat him like a king."

"I know," I mumbled. And I put my finger through the bars of the cage and petted Rodent so that I wouldn't have to look at her. "Bye Rodent," I said. "See you in two weeks."

At home, Kate was singing, "We're all going on a … summer holiday … a summer holiday with youwhowho who…" as she tried to close her very stuffed suitcase.

"Sit up there, fatso," she said to me. So I sat up on the case and squashed down the lid and she somehow managed to pull the zip shut without bursting the whole thing.

"Why can't Dad come too?" I suddenly blurted out. Even as I said it, I knew that it was a stupid thing to say.

Kate stopped what she was doing and stared at me as if I had lost my marbles.

"Are you serious?" she said.

"No. Forget it!" I said crossly and walked out of the room. I wished that I had never opened my big mouth. But, of course, Kate wouldn't forget it and followed me.

"It would be a disaster, Tao," she called out. "We would fight all the time. You know that."

I did know that.

"Do you not like Paul?" she called out. I don't know why she said that.

"Yes, I do," I shouted. And I do. He's really nice.

"Do you not want to go on this holiday?" she asked, chasing down the stairs after me.

"Yes, I do!" I yelled crossly. "Just leave me alone!" And I marched out into the garden and slammed the back door after me.

Kate didn't follow. She just stood in the kitchen with a puzzled look on her face, wondering what had come over me. *I* didn't know what had come over me, so how could she know?

Later as I was lying in bed, I heard her talking to Paul on the phone. I couldn't catch everything she said because her voice was very low, just a few words here and there.

"Out of the blue ... no, no, it's not you ... thought he had got over all that ... it's been a rollercoaster few months for both of them ... probably overexcitement..."

Sometimes it seems to me that adults blame every-thing children do on "overexcitement". Especially when they are the ones who are overexcited.

"If my dad doesn't come back to Kate soon," I said out loud to Rodent, "it will be too late." Which was really silly, because Rodent wasn't even there.

Then my phone beeped.

cya tomorrow can't
wait Mimi XXX

Suddenly, I couldn't understand why I had got so upset. I really was looking forward to this holiday. Maybe I *had* just got a bit overexcited?

Before we left for the airport the next morning, I rooted around in the shoebox under my bed, the one that is full of junk, until I found the crumpled-up envelope with the wolf charm that Jo had given me. Then I opened the zip on my suitcase just enough to slip it in. I'm not sure why I did that.

Chapter 21

The first evening in the holiday house was fine. The trouble only really started the next day. And that was because of the rain.

The house was in the west of Ireland. In front of the house was the sea and a little beach. Behind the house was a lake and big mountains. It was a sunny evening when Kate and I got there and it looked like a postcard.

"This is a little piece of heaven," declared Kate, clapping her hands together. The Roches had already arrived and Paul and Mimi were making a big dinner for everyone. They had a book called *The Idiot's Cookbook* and Mimi was in charge of reading out the instructions. Sparkler was jumping all over me and

Kate in her excitement.

"Heat the oven to gas mark seven, idiot!" she shouted at Paul. "Sit, Sparkler!" she shouted at Sparkler, who ignored her, of course.

"It's an electric oven, idiot!" he called back. "The dog is an idiot too," he said to us.

"Then put it to 220 degrees, idiot!" she shouted at him, trying not to laugh.

Conor had gone to the shop on the bike to get milk and stuff. Paul told Mimi that she was no help at all and to take me and that fool of a dog for a look around, while Kate – if she didn't mind helping – and he got on with the dinner. Sally was nowhere to be seen.

"She's lying on her bunk reading her stupid book and she's in her usual rotten mood," Mimi explained while we walked along the beach. "I wouldn't go near her, Tao."

"Why is she in a bad mood?" I asked.

"God only knows," said Mimi, rolling her eyes to heaven. "Probably because I bagsed the top bunk. And she didn't want to come."

"Why not?"

"Oh, you know … the usual stuff," Mimi answered vaguely. "She didn't want to leave her dirty hens behind and her precious vegetable patch even though George said he'd come over every day to look after them."

We took off our sandals and went for a paddle, but the water was so cold. Sparkler didn't seem to mind. We threw stones for her and she charged into the water and then came out and shook herself all over us.

"Go away, Sparkler," I shouted at her. She ignored me, of course.

"Tomorrow we can go for a swim," said Mimi, "and dig a hole to China!"

"It's a long way down, Mimi," I said.

"We could visit our Chinese mum and dad," she said, ignoring my comment. "Do you ever wonder about them, Tao?" she asked me.

I picked up a flat stone and tried to skim it on the sea, but it sank after only three hops.

"Sometimes," I said.

"Imagine," said Mimi, trying to skim a big round stone, which was never going to work, "if my dad married your mum, then you would have three mums, counting Kate and Jo and your Chinese mum, and two dads, counting mine and yours. No, three if you count your Chinese dad. And I would have three dads counting my dad and your dad and my Chinese dad, and two mums, counting Kate and my Chinese mum. Three, if you count my mum, who is dead. Four, if you count Jo. It's mad, isn't it, Tao ... when you think about it?" she finished.

"You can't count Jo," I told her.

"Why not?" said Mimi.

"Because…" I said, but I didn't really know how to say it. "Because … she doesn't count," I finished flatly.

Mimi said, "You think she stole your daddy away, don't you?"

"She did," I said. "We were fine, me and Dad and Kate, before Jo came along."

"You can't just blame Jo," argued Mimi, flinging another fat stone into the sea with a splash. " How do you make those stones hop?"

"You have to use flat ones," I explained, skimming another stone for about five hops. "I blame Jo because it was all her fault. If she hadn't got a job in Dad's office, he would still live with us."

Mimi didn't answer. She was looking for a flat stone, but I knew she didn't agree with me.

"I'd love it if my dad married Kate," she said, "because she's really nice, you know."

Well, I did know that, but it gave me a warm feeling when Mimi said it.

"I miss having a mammy," she said sadly. She threw her stone, but it just sank like all the others. She sighed loudly.

"You couldn't dig all the way to China anyway," I told her, because I wanted to change the subject.

"No, s'pose not," agreed Mimi, but she didn't sound convinced. "Anyway, if you did you would fall out of the sky when you got there and probably die."

"No, you wouldn't." I couldn't help laughing. "You'd come out on the ground even on the bottom of the world."

Mimi bit her lip while she thought about that. Then she shook her head and giggled. "Then everyone in China would be walking around upside down!"

Now I was confused. So we tried to walk upside down on our hands, the Chinese way, but neither of us were very good at it and in the end we just lay flat on our backs on the sand and laughed and tried to stop Sparkler from licking our faces until Paul and Kate arrived to call us giddy-goats in for dinner. Kate had her arm linked in Paul's.

The next day, it rained cats and dogs.

Chapter 22

"I'm bored! There is nothing to do here," said Sally. "There's not even a telly."

"Relax, Sally," said Paul. "Why don't you all play a big game of Monopoly?"

"Yes!" said Mimi. "I'll get it." And she ran off to her bedroom.

I liked the sound of that, too. I'm a champion at Monopoly.

"I don't want to play bloody Monopoly!" shouted Sally. "I'm going for a walk."

"Well, take your coat," said Kate.

"You are not my mother!" snapped back Sally and stormed out the door, slamming it so hard behind her that the whole house shook.

"Sally!" shouted Paul, jumping up and marching towards the door. He looked really cross.

"Leave it, Paul," Kate called after him. "She's right. I shouldn't have opened my big mouth."

Paul stopped and stood still for a few moments.

"It's not acceptable behaviour," he said. "I'll be having a strong word with that young madam when she gets back."

Conor looked at me and rolled his eyes.

"Looks like World War III has just broken out," he said and grinned.

But Paul wasn't laughing. And neither was Kate. Her face was bright red. She bit into the toast she was holding and that's when her filling fell out.

"Ow!" she moaned.

Paul insisted on driving Kate to a dentist even though she said that there was no need, that she'd pop a pain-killer and she'd be fine, but he didn't want it to spoil her holiday so off they went. Conor and Mimi and I played Monopoly because there was no point in everybody going. Sally still wasn't back and Kate was worried that she might be completely soaked, but Paul said that it was her own fault and served her right for being so rude.

Sometimes it seems to me that every house has

different rules for Monopoly. If we had played Kate and my rules I would probably have won, but Mimi and Conor had some rules all of their own. So I lost ... for the first time ever.

Firstly, their board had Dublin streets, not London streets.

Secondly, Mimi bagsed the racing car first, which is my lucky piece that Kate always lets me use, so I got stuck with the top hat, which turned out to be a very unlucky piece.

Thirdly, Conor and Mimi didn't let you take loans from the bank when you needed money, even if you promised you would pay it back when you passed Go.

Fourthly, they showed no mercy. If you couldn't pay the amount, they NEVER let you off.

No wonder I was first out. I was really fed up about that.

"I don't like your rules," I said and threw my unlucky top hat back in the box with a clatter.

"So who do you normally play against, Tao?" asked Conor as he sorted all the money and the houses and the hotels that I had just given him. I had nothing at all left.

"Kate," I said.

"And does she always let you win?" He laughed, throwing the dice.

"No, she does not!" I answered crossly, and I was glad to see him land on Shrewsbury Road (which is the Irish version of Oxford Street), which Mimi owned and had a hotel on.

"Yes!" she cried, punching the air. She was the luckiest player I've ever seen. She owned about three-quarters of the board and had a big messy mountain of money in a heap in front of her.

"Cough up the cash, loser," she said. Conor sighed.

It was clear that he was going to lose, but it was going to take a while yet. I wandered out into the garden. The rain had stopped and there was even a bit of blue sky opening up. Sally had come back. I had heard her having a shower. Sparkler was asleep in her basket in the kitchen. I walked down to the lake, where the boat was tied up.

Paul said that he'd take us out fishing in the boat when the rain stopped. Well, the rain had stopped, but he wasn't here. What was taking them so long anyway, I wondered.

"They've probably gone off and got married," I said out loud into the wind. Which was a really stupid thing to say, but I didn't care.

I climbed into the boat and sat in the middle seat. I wasn't going to go anywhere – anyway, there were no oars. I just wanted to be on my own for a bit and be grouchy and I liked the way the boat bobbed gently up and down on the water. There was nobody about, so I could talk away out loud to myself.

"How dare Conor say that Kate lets me win," I told the lake. "What does he know, anyway? He's not so good himself. Mimi is going to whup his ass!"

I liked saying that. "Whup his ass." I repeated it in my American accent that David says sounds like a drunk Eskimo. As if he knows what a drunk Eskimo sounds like. Anyway, Kalem says they are called Inuits now.

"And another thing," I told the sky, "Sally's right – Kate is not her mother. She's my mother. But if Kate and Paul want to get married, well, I don't care. I can just go and live with Dad and Jo and the twins, can't I?"

"And Mimi can come and live with us if she likes," I continued. The wind was strong and there was no one about to hear me. "Or maybe we can go back to China. Even if we have to dig all the way." Which even though I was cross made me smile as I thought of us popping out of a hole in the middle of China all covered in dirt and all these Chinese people standing on their heads with their mouths dropping open.

In fact, I wasn't really as cross as I was trying to be, but it felt good to be complaining out loud.

Maybe if I hadn't been complaining so much,

I would have noticed that the rope had come loose and the boat was drifting away from the bank.

That's when I really should have started shouting properly, but at first, it didn't seem so serious. I probably could have stepped out of the boat and paddled to the edge but I hesitated because I didn't want to get my feet wet and, before I knew it the boat had drifted way out onto the lake.

Now I shouted for help as loud as I could but the wind blew my voice away and pushed the boat further and further from the shore. The boat had no oars and kept turning in circles and the little bobbing waves were a lot choppier out here. I hadn't even got a life jacket on. I sat frozen to the spot on the middle seat, holding tightly to the sides as the boat drifted across the grey lake.

Where was everybody? Why wasn't the boat properly tied up? Why was I finding it hard to breathe? I thought I might jump in and swim to the shore but I was too afraid.

"Help! Help!" I screamed. I tried to stand up but the boat wobbled so much I had to sit back down or fall in. I tried to keep my head and stay calm but it's hard to keep your head when you are going to drown!

"Help!" I screamed, and tears started pouring down my face. Where was everybody? Was there nobody left in the world to save me? I could see my mobile phone on the floor beside my bed – why hadn't I taken it with me?

I tried to think what Dad would do. He always kept his cool in a crisis. I took a deep breath and told myself to calm down. Relax. But it was easier said than done and the stupid boat just went round and round although at least it wasn't sinking. Someone will come soon, I told myself. Just stay in the boat. And yell!

"Help! Help!" But the wind just blew my yells up into the sky, even if there had been someone about to hear me.

After what seemed like ages, the boat drifted right across the lake, which wasn't very big, and thumped into the bank on the far side. Which meant I was safe. I climbed out and stood on the soft mossy bank and looked back across at our house. My legs felt wobbly, but I didn't care. I was still alive. All I had to do was walk back around the lake and think up a good excuse for what happened. The sun had come out and it was already hard to remember why I had felt so frightened.

Chapter 23

The sun didn't stay out for long. I hadn't got very far when a damp mist came in from the sea and covered it up. I could no longer see the other side of the lake, but I knew if I followed the lake shore I would get back to the house in the end. It was just that the ground was very boggy and my shoes kept sinking into the mud. I tried to step on tufts of grass, but it meant I was taking a long time.

I wondered if they'd noticed that I was gone yet. Was Kate back and going hysterical? Had they seen that the boat was missing? Were there search teams out looking for me yet?

Probably not. Mimi and Conor were probably still

playing Monopoly, while Sally sulked in her bedroom and Kate and Paul were still at the dentist. I was all alone in the world and nobody cared.

Then suddenly I was standing at the edge of a river. A fast river flowing into the lake. I hadn't expected that. It had just appeared out of the mist. I didn't know what to do. Should I try to cross and maybe drown or walk all the way back around the lake the other way? I was getting cold and my clothes were all wet from the mist and I was sick of walking. I didn't want to go back all the way that I had come, but I was afraid of the rushing river. I had come too far to drown now. Maybe there were stepping stones further on or somewhere I could cross safely.

I began walking up the side of the river. It was hard going because the ground climbed steeply and soon I was walking through trees. They looked creepy in the grey mist, reaching down their branches to slap my face and tripping me up with their roots. A bird burst out in front of me and my heart nearly jumped out of my chest.

It was getting harder and harder to follow the windy river. There were rocks and brambles along its edge, and the mountain I was climbing, which seemed middle-sized when I looked at it from the house, was getting steeper and steeper. I couldn't help it. I started to cry.

Maybe I should have tried to go on a bit further, but I was getting panicky. I had to get across that river. Now or never. There were some rocks in it that I could jump onto.

My first jump was nearly my last. I just about reached the edge of a flat rock sticking out of the rushing water but I almost fell backwards. I took a moment to get my nerve back and then jumped onto the next rock. This was a much shorter jump, but there was slimy, green stuff on the rock that was very slippy and my feet slid off it. I had to grab on with both hands, my legs hanging in the river. Frantically, I pulled myself up onto the slippery, green stone. My legs were bleeding and I was soaking.

I made a last big jump for the other side and managed to catch hold of the grassy edge with my hands and dragged myself up out of the river.

I had made it! I was a complete mess, but I was safely across. It was straightforward now. Down the mountain I ran. I couldn't wait to get home. They must be sick with worry. Kate was probably screaming her head off. Dad says she doesn't know the meaning of calm. Paul would be beside himself, whatever that means, and Mimi and Conor were probably running around like headless chickens shouting, "Tao Tao!"

Sally … well, Sally was probably reading in her bedroom with her headphones on.

You shouldn't run down a mountain. Even when you can't wait to get home. Because you can trip and twist your ankle or maybe even break your leg. Without warning, my left foot went into a hole and I tumbled forward and hit my head hard on a rock. I didn't remember anything after that.

Chapter 24

When I woke up, I didn't know where I was. There was a bad pain shooting all around my head and I closed my eyes again. It wasn't just my head that ached. My foot was in agony too. Slowly I opened my eyes again and a big fat yellow moon was looking down at me. It was night-time and I was lying on the side of a mountain and I was all on my own. Oh, God!

I tried to stand up, but my foot wouldn't hold me. I screamed in pain and fell back down again. I was so frightened. My tummy felt like it was being squeezed by giant hands and I thought that I would throw up. Then a cloud covered the moon and I couldn't even see my own hands.

"Helphelphelp! Someonehelpme!" I screamed and screamed but no one answered. "Help me, please!" I cried and my face was all wet with tears. I felt so little and so lonely. And so scared.

There was a noise in the grass near me. The moon still hadn't come out, but my eyes were getting a bit used to the blackness – I could just make out the dark shapes of big trees waving their branches in the wind as if they were alive. I never knew that trees could be scary. Then there was that noise in the grass again. A small animal noise. Were there snakes in Ireland? I didn't know. I stayed dead still. The noise stopped, but what did that mean? Was I about to be bitten by a viper or an anaconda that I couldn't even see? A long time passed. I was sweating, but I was very cold too. And wet.

There was something moving about over there near the trees. It was an animal. I couldn't see it, but I could hear it. I wished Kate was here to give me a hug … even if she wasn't cool in a crisis. But nobody was here. Except me. They were all home in their beds. Except me. I had never felt so terrified in all my life. There were wild animals prowling around. And snakes in the grass. Probably rats, too.

Hours passed. Well, it felt like hours. I got colder and

colder. The moon went in and out of the clouds and I kept falling asleep and waking up. This night was going to go on for ever. I didn't hear the snake anymore. Perhaps it had gone away. Or was it just waiting?

Then I heard the helicopter. Its big blades were whirring somewhere far off. And then I could see it – it had a big strong spotlight shining down on the mountainside. I waved my arms about and shouted, but the noise of the helicopter was too loud. Round and round it flew, but the spotlight never shone on me.

"I'M HERE! I'M HERE!" I yelled, but it was no use. In the end, the helicopter flew off in the other direction and gradually its noise got weaker and weaker, and I was all alone again.

Had they had given up and left me to die?

I imagined Kate finding me cold and dead in the morning and carrying my lifeless body down the mountain. Everybody crying their eyes out. Especially Mimi. Everyone saying what a lovely boy I was and what a sad way to go. All because of a game of Monopoly.

I felt so tired. My eyes began to close and I began to drift away.

Chapter 25

Then the Head Honcho started shouting at me.

"Stop feeling so sorry for yourself you miserable, pathetic, lily-livered excuse for a centre-half!"

My eyes flew open. Suddenly I was wide awake. I looked all around, but there was no sign of the Head Honcho … or anybody else. The big yellow moon made the world look silver. Over by the trees, I saw the animal. It was a wolf. Standing very still. Looking at me.

"Follow the wolf, Tao!" the Head Honcho roared in my head.

"Are you mad?" I answered out loud, but I was beginning to think that I might be the one going mad.

What was the Head Honcho doing in my head? Kalem says that the last voice a person hears before they die is the voice of the one they love the most. And I was hearing the Head Honcho? Perhaps I wasn't about to die.

"The wolf only kills those who fear it," said Willy in that drawling way of his. He was in my head, too.

"Where did you steal that one from, Willy?" I asked the Willy in my head. All the time, I kept my eyes on that wolf.

The wolf had half-turned, as if to say follow me. I don't know why, but I started to pull myself up. Very slowly, I placed my sore foot on the ground – terrible pains shot like long needles up my leg. I steadied myself and, clenching my fists, took a step in the direction of the wolf. Which made no sense at all.

"Go on, go on, go on," urged the Head Honcho. "Remember what I always say. No guts, no glory."

So I took another step and another. Each time I put my sore foot on the ground, I felt like screaming. The wolf moved a little further away into the trees and waited. I knew he meant me to follow.

"In your true heart, you are a wolf," said Jo. Was she in my head too? It was getting crowded in there.

And so I slowly followed that big grey wolf into the wood and down a narrow track, silver in the light of the moon, and I had no idea where I was going or what would happen to me. Every so often, the wolf would stop and wait while I caught up, but as soon as I got nearer to him, he would move off again.

Whenever I felt like giving up and lying down on the forest floor, the voices in my head would start up again. And now it wasn't just the Head Honcho and Willy and Jo – it was lots of people that I knew.

"When the going gets tough, the tough go shopping!" said David. It was one of his favourite sayings and I smiled when I heard it in my head ... but I kept going.

I was dizzy and it was hard to keep my eyes open. When I put my hand on the back of my head, it was wet and sticky. But still the wolf led me on and still the moon lit the way.

I tripped on a root and fell off the path into heather. I blacked out for a minute. When I came round, every muscle in my body was screaming, "Stop! Stop!" My foot was killing me, I was sure that it was broken. Everything looked blurry. The heather was soft like a bed. I just wanted to sleep.

"Don't be such a sissy, Tao!" roared the Head Honcho. "Football is a game of two halves. Now get back in the game!"

I wished he'd shut up.

"My brother doesn't give up," said Mimi, who had obviously decided to join the people in my head. "Use the stick under your hand, Tao."

Which was a lot more useful advice than the raving of the Head Honcho, because there was a stick under my right arm.

"OK, OK," I told the voices crossly and, using the stick, I pulled myself up out of the heather and got ready to follow my wolf guide once more.

The wolf was waiting the same distance ahead and looking straight at me. A wolf has weird eyes.

"To look into the eyes of the wolf is to see your own soul," said Willy.

"Another one you stole, Willy, I suppose?" I told him, but I started walking again. It was still very difficult, but the walking stick helped me to keep the weight off my sore foot.

"Dig deep, Tao," said my dad, "not far to go."

That helped, even if I had no idea where I was going.

"As I always say," joined in the Head Honcho, who really did not know when to be quiet, "show me a good loser and I'll show you an idiot!"

"You stole that!" popped in Willy, sounding very cross.

"You're the one to talk," fired back the Head Honcho.

Oh, for flip's sake ... now the voices in my head were having a row. I was distracted by it and I didn't notice straight away that the wolf had disappeared. I stopped walking and looked all around, but there was no sign of him. I felt panicky. I had lost my guide... Then I saw that the end of the forest path was just ahead and it came out onto a road, black tarmac shining in the moonlight.

I moved on as quickly as I could (which wasn't very quickly), until I reached the road. I looked up and down but, of course, there was no one about at that hour. I leant back against a big tree that stood beside the road and slid slowly down its smooth trunk until I was sitting. Then I waited.

The sky was more blue-black than black-black now and far away, where it touched the ground, was a line of white light. The long night was coming to an end. The tree felt warm and strong against my back.

"Hug a tree and it will hug you back," Kate's voice whispered in my head. I didn't feel so frightened anymore. Somebody would surely find me soon. I let my eyes close slowly ... and nobody started shouting in my head.

Chapter 26

I woke up in a hospital. I found out later that a mountain rescue team had found me sitting against the tree and had phoned for an ambulance. I didn't remember anything about that at all.

Now everything felt muzzy, like I was swimming underwater trying to reach the surface. I could hear voices, but it took me a few moments to recognize who was talking. It was Kate and Dad ... and they were arguing. I kept my eyes shut. They thought that I was still asleep.

"You shouldn't have left the children on their own," Dad was whispering loudly. He sounded very angry. "Where were you, anyway?"

"I was at the dentist," answered Kate, and she was whispering too. I could hear a catch in her voice. "My filling fell out."

"Oh, for God's sake!" hissed Dad. "He's only ten. We could have lost him. You do realize that, don't you? All alone on that mountain all night long."

"Yes, I do know that," said Kate, and I could hear her sobbing and sniffling.

Maybe I should have opened my eyes then, but I felt so sad to hear my mum and dad fighting like that. A memory of a Christmas Day long ago when they were still together floated into my head. Both of them were trying very hard to be nice to me, but they were not talking to each other. I could still feel the horrible pain in my tummy that I felt all that day. Everyone pretending to be happy. Why couldn't they be just a bit nicer to each other like other mums and dads?

"I'm going for a coffee," said Dad. "Call me if he wakes up." The door closed loudly then and the only sound in the room was Kate crying quietly. I could feel her hand on mine and I drifted back to sleep.

The next voice I heard was Paul's.

"Stop beating yourself up about it, Kate," he was saying. His voice was gentle and calm. "It was not your fault."

"James is right," Kate whimpered. "We should have taken the children with us."

"He's upset," said Paul. "He'll calm down. He got a bad fright. We all did. Come on, blow your nose. That brave boy of yours is going to wake up any minute and you don't want him to see you like that, do you?"

I sneaked a peep while Kate blew her nose loudly into a tissue that Paul handed her.

"Look at me," Paul said and Kate turned her face to him with a funny, crooked smile. "You are a good mother," he told her, saying each word slowly and clearly. While he was talking, he was wiping away her tears with his fingers, which was making an even worse mess of her face. Then Kate buried her head in his shoulder and he held her and stroked her hair. I tried to feel cross, but I just wasn't able to.

It is a funny feeling waking up after you have had an operation. Your brain feels like a fluffy cloud and you have to concentrate very hard on what you want to say. Or you might just say the first thing that comes into your head.

"You two should get married," I said and opened my eyes.

They both pulled apart and looked at me. Kate's mouth fell open and her eyes looked like they would pop out of her head.

"You're awake!" she shouted, and nearly jumped into the bed with me. Her hug was the nicest thing I had ever felt. But it hurt!

"Oh, I'msorryI'msorryI'msorry," she said, kissing me all over my face.

Then she jumped up.

"I'll go and get James," she said in a rush, but Paul stopped her and said he'd go.

Before he left, Paul squeezed my hand and said, "Good to have you back, Tao."

Chapter 27

Kate said that the wolf was my spirit guide. Dad said that that was a load of codswallop. There had been no wolves in Ireland for at least five hundred years.

"Well, how do you explain it then?" asked Kate.

"I don't know," said Dad, which wasn't like him. "Tao had a bang on his head. It could have been a fox … or else he was seeing things. He was concussed after all."

"It was a wolf, Dad," I told him. Kate gave everyone standing around the bed her I-told-you-so look.

Dad sighed and dropped the subject. He was in a good mood now that I was awake again and sitting up in bed with a big plaster on my ankle and a bandage wrapped around my head, eating my dinner.

"You look like an axe murderer," said Mimi and everyone laughed.

My phone beeped again. This time it was a text from Kalem's mum.

> From Zero to Hero!
> Get well soon. Love
> and pinches, Angela
> xx PS Tell Kate
> that Willy is already
> busy working on a
> Willyism for you ...
> more damn graffiti
> all over the café!

I had already got texts from Kalem and David.

David said I should go on television because "I'm a celebrity".

Kalem texted me a joke to cheer me up...

> Did u hear bt d
> man who was tap
> dancing?
> He broke his ankle
> when he fell into the
> sink. LOL

"I get it!" shouted Mimi and everybody laughed, except Sally, who turned her eyes to heaven.

Jo had rung to tell me, "that I was a scallywag and that I had given everyone an awful fright and sorry but she was finding it very hard to talk without crying but they were tears of joy because I was OK and she hadn't said anything to the twins because they wouldn't understand and that she loved me but she'd kill me when she saw me for pulling such a stunt and—"

"Jo," I interrupted her.

"Yes?"

"Thank you for the charm."

She was quiet for a moment after that, but I could hear her sniffling.

"Just so long as you are safe," she said eventually.

Sally told me that she had run away once too.

"I didn't run away," I said.

"Whatever. Just don't do it again."

Conor told me that he just wanted to let me know that this wasn't going to make any difference to how we played Monopoly. Then he grinned and threw a present of a pair of Wolves socks at me, "even though they suck!"

Mimi hugged me and said that I was a wally and that I was to take her with me next time I set off on one of my adventures.

Before Dad flew home, he visited me on his own. It was my last day in the hospital. He told me that he would ring me at least once a day until I was sick of the sound of his voice. He also said that he was very proud of me. Then he told me he loved me and if anything bad had happened to me on that mountain he would never, ever ... but his voice all choked up then and he couldn't finish the sentence. He gave me a quick hug and told me to take care. He'd see me again at the end of next week. Then he walked quickly out of the room without looking back.

A few seconds later, the door opened and he stuck his head back into the room.

"One last thing, Tao," he called. "It was a fox." And his head popped out the door again.

"It was a wolf!" I shouted after him. I could hear his big laugh as his footsteps disappeared down the corridor.

"Fox!" he shouted.

"Wolf!" I shouted back and I could hear whoever was in the next room joining in the laughter.

I lay back on the pillows and smiled to myself. I was glad that I hadn't mentioned the voices in my head.

Kate and Paul collected me to drive me back to the

holiday house. Mimi couldn't come because I had to stretch out my leg along the back seat. Paul lifted me into the car and put my crutches on the floor.

It was a lovely sunny drive and I was glad to be out of the hospital. Kate kept turning around in her seat and patting my hand and smiling.

"Do you remember the first thing you said when you came out of the anaesthetic, Tao?" asked Paul out of the blue. He sounded mischievous.

I felt my face go red. I looked out the window. I could see the mountain that I had spent the night on in the distance. It looked soft and green and not a bit scary in the sunshine. I wondered what my wolf was doing.

"Well?" said Paul again.

Kate said nothing, but she was sitting very still.

"No," I said and I laughed a little. "I can't remember."

Paul threw his head back and laughed loudly.

"Funny that," he said. "I can't either." He patted Kate's knee. She turned her head and gave me a funny grin. Her eyes were smiling. But she didn't say anything.

Part 3

Chapter 28

It was a big relief to get the cast taken off my ankle five weeks after the holiday was over. The best thing was to be able to give my foot a good scratch.

"There is nothing worse than an itchy foot that you can't scratch," I told Rodent, who was having a big scratch himself.

The Head Honcho was very pleased, even though it would be another few weeks before the muscles in my foot were strong enough for football.

"The only player I have with a half-decent left foot and he goes and breaks it in the off-season," he had said when he found out, and had thrown his arms up to the heavens.

I had made the big mistake of telling Kalem and David about hearing the Head Honcho's voice in my head when I was lost on the mountain.

"Hearing voices in your head is the first sign of madness," said David.

"Is there hair growing on the palms of your hands yet? Because that's the second sign," added Kalem.

Without thinking, I looked at the palms of my hands. Another mistake.

"And checking your palms is the third sign!" whooped Kalem and they both fell about the place as if it was the biggest joke.

"You're a looper," jeered David, and jumped out of the way when I swung my crutch at him.

I had got very used to my crutch, but it had been a bit of a nuisance during the holiday. It kept sinking in the sand when we went to the beach and I fell over quite a lot.

"Here we go again," Conor would say as he pulled me up. "My wobbly little brother topples over once more."

It didn't stop me going in the water though. Paul taped this big black plastic binbag over my cast to keep it dry and I managed to splash about. But it was very hard to actually swim, even though the cast did feel lighter in the water.

The sun shone every day after I left the hospital and everybody was in a much better mood. Even Sally.

The best day was the fishing trip. Kate didn't come because boats were not her thing and Sally could think of nothing more boring than sitting about waiting for a fish to bite, so they went off together to visit some sort of open organic farm.

"Talk about boring," said Mimi, but I think they enjoyed themselves because they came back with seeds and catalogues and stuff and spent the whole of dinner making plans for Sally's vegetable patch, when they weren't teasing us.

"Not even one miserable little fish," sneered Sally. "All day in a boat and you can't even bring home one miserable little fish."

Kate snorted with laughter when Sally said that, which started everyone off.

"Oh, but you should have seen the one that got away," said Paul and stretched his hands out to show how big the imaginary fish that got away was.

"Got thrown away more like," blurted out Conor, giving Mimi a look.

The truth is that we did catch three fish, but Mimi always found a reason to throw them back.

"That one is a baby," she said about the first one that Conor caught. It was small all right, flopping around the bottom of the boat. "Its mammy will miss it. You should throw it back, Conor."

Conor wasn't too pleased, but he threw it back. Maybe he didn't fancy killing it either.

The fish I caught was a big one. It was so exciting. I had been sitting there for ages, my rod hanging out the back of the boat and my broken foot propped up on the middle seat, while Paul rowed the boat across the lake.

"We're taking the oars with us this time," he'd said to me and winked as we pushed off. We had life jackets on this time, too.

The lake was much calmer than on the day when I nearly drowned and the sky was completely blue.

The fish took me by surprise.

"I've got one!" I yelled when the rod was nearly pulled out of my hand. "And it's a big mother…"

Paul threw back his head and laughed and stuck the oars firmly in the water to steady the boat.

"Hold on tight, Tao," said Mimi.

"Reel him in. Reel him in," called Conor. The rod was bending so much that I thought it would break and I could barely turn the reel.

"It's the Loch Ness Monster!" shouted Mimi, who was so excited that Paul had to tell her to sit still or she'd turn over the boat.

"Hardly … seeing as this isn't even Loch Ness," Conor told her sarcastically. He had to help me hold the rod and try to reel in the fish, who was beginning to get tired and not fighting so much. Mimi had the net and was dangling it over the side ready for action. Paul was doing his best to keep the boat steady and shouting encouragement at me.

"He's a wily old fish, Tao, you've got to play him. Feed him some line," he called out. "Now reel him in. Mimi, scoop him up with the net."

"Yes!" I shouted.

And there he was. A huge fish … well, a quite big fish … thrashing about on the floor of the boat, and I had caught him all by myself … with only a little help.

Conor took the oars while Paul took the hook out of the fish's mouth.

"Ah, the poor thing," said Mimi. "It's probably the daddy of my baby fish."

"So what?" said Conor sharply.

"Well, we can't kill it, can we?" she said. "It's too cruel."

"Well, Tao?" sighed Paul. "It's up to you. It's your fish."

I looked at the fish and its small beady eye looked back at me.

"I don't care," I said, but I did a bit. "I don't really

like fish, anyway. Throw him back."

Mimi was happy about that, but Conor threw his eyes to heaven as Paul, with a funny smile, carefully put the fish back into the water.

"Well, that's just great." Conor sounded fed up.

"We will keep the next one. Promise," said Mimi.

Mimi caught the next one. It wasn't huge like mine, but it was quite big and she nearly fell out of the boat in excitement.

"OK, we'll keep this one," she declared as Conor took out the hook.

"We will not!" said Conor, and he chucked Mimi's fish back into the lake.

"Why did you do that?" shouted Mimi.

"Because it's probably the wife of Tao's fish or the best friend of my fish or the king of the fishes in this lake or—"

"All right," interrupted Mimi. "I get the message, Conor. You're really mean, you know that?" she finished crossly. But Conor just grinned at her.

"It's like those tales of three wishes where they waste them all," said Kate, cutting her fish finger in half. "The Tale of the Three Fishes."

When I went to Dad and Jo's house the twins wanted to hear the Tale of the Three Fishes again and then we had to act it out. The couch was the boat and I was Conor and Roger was me and Rachel was Mimi and the cushions all over the floor were fish. It made a change from *Mary Poppins* and, as usual, it ended up in a cushion fight.

Later, when the twins were in bed, Dad said that he and Jo had something to tell me. They both looked serious but happy at the same time. Dad was holding Jo's hand, which he doesn't normally do.

"Don't look so worried, Tao," smiled Jo. "It's not bad news."

We were all sitting in the living room. I wasn't really sure I liked these adult "talks" very much.

"You tell him, Jo," said Dad, which didn't make me feel any better.

Jo blushed and then she took a deep breath and said, "Your father and I are getting married. That's it. That's our big news."

I opened my mouth and closed it again.

"You look like one of those fish you threw back," said Dad.

"It's just that…" I stuttered. "I mean … does that mean that…?"

But I didn't ask the question. Dad's whole face was smiling and Jo's eyes were twinkling. Jo guessed my question, but she guessed wrong.

"Don't worry," she said, putting her hand on mine. "It will make no difference in the world to you. This will always be your other home. It's just that I will now officially be your wicked stepmother."

"So does that answer your question, Tao?" asked Dad.

Well, it didn't because that wasn't my question. I was going to ask did it mean that Dad would never get back with Kate now. It was a bit of a stupid question and in the end I was glad that I hadn't asked it. Because I already knew the answer and it somehow didn't seem so important any more.

"Yes," I said.

Jo smiled her big kind smile. "So how about a hug?"

She opened her arms to me and there was a "please" in her eyes. I hesitated a moment.

"Only if you want to," she said quietly.

I did want to. So I gave Jo a hug and then I hugged Dad. If I am not careful, I will turn into a serial hugger, just like Kate.

Dad opened a bottle of champagne to celebrate and Jo put a cushion over her face when the cork shot out, because she was afraid it would hit her and take her eye out, but it just belted off the ceiling and the champagne bubbled out of the bottle.

"Just as well the twins would sleep through an earthquake," said Dad and he poured me a small glass of champagne, but I didn't like it at all, especially the way the bubbles went up my nose.

"I've a bottle of 7UP in the fridge," said Jo, and went to get me some.

"I told Kate this morning," said Dad, when Jo was in the kitchen. "She's OK with it. Are you OK with it?"

I didn't answer straight away. I tried hard to remember why I had always dreaded this day and I couldn't. Jo came back and handed me a glass of 7UP.

"Yes," I said. "I'm OK with it."

Then we all clinked our glasses and drank a toast to Jo and Dad.

"And Tao," added Jo.

I don't remember ever seeing Dad look so happy.

Chapter 29

"Dad and Jo are getting married," was the first thing that I said to Kate when I saw her. "He said that he told you."

"He did," said Kate, looking up from her book. Rodent was sleeping on her lap. "About time, too. They were always a better couple than we were. Your dad and I never saw eye to eye."

She was smiling. She didn't mind. She didn't mind at all. "Did you hear the big news?" she said.

That was an odd thing to say.

"Yes," I said slowly. "I just told you…"

"No. Not that," she laughed. "Marigold had her baby."

I must have looked confused because she added

quickly, "You know, Mimi's Aunt M ... the one who was pregnant."

I remembered then, all right. I had put my hands on her big fat tummy.

Then the phone rang.

"Oh, that will be Mimi," said Kate. "She's dying to tell you herself. I told her when you'd be back."

It was Mimi.

"It's a boy," she said. "Can you believe it? He weighs ten pounds. That's absolutely tiny. But you're not the baby's uncle, after all, and I wouldn't have been an Aunt M even if it had been a girl, because Aunt M is my mum's sister. It's very confusing."

I had to agree with her there.

"It turns out the baby is my cousin and..." She went quiet for a minute to build up the excitement. "He's your cousin, too!"

A stepmum and a new cousin in one day. My family was growing bigger by the minute.

"What's his name?" I asked, but Mimi said that he had no name yet because Aunt M and Nicholas were so sure that it was going to be a girl and then they were going to call it Poppy or Petal, but there weren't many boys called after flowers. Nicholas says that they are open to suggestions.

"You might think of a name, Tao," said Mimi, all

excited. "You named Scottie and that's the other big news. Scottie laid her first organic egg this morning. Sally ate it."

I laughed when I heard that. Then Mimi said that Paul was clearing out the spare room with all the junk in it and they were going to make it into a bedroom just for me, Tao, because I was part of their family now and their home was my home and her grandad was carving a name plate for the door that says: Tao's Room. Wasn't that great?

It was great. I had three homes and three families. Christmas was going to be amazing.

Then it was my turn to tell Mimi about Dad and Jo.

"I thought that they were married already," said Mimi. "Next thing, my dad and your Kate will be getting married, I bet you!"

I remembered Kate's look when Paul was teasing me on the way home from the hospital about what I had said when I awoke from the anaesthetic.

"I'd love it if they did," added Mimi.

"Me too," I said. It just popped out. But it was true.

Kate and I had one of our long chats before I went to bed. Kate calls them "heart-to-hearts". There was a lot to talk about and it was all good. The radio was playing quietly in the background. We weren't listening to it, but suddenly a song caught my attention.

"Who sings that?" I asked Kate, and I walked across to the radio and turned it up.

"Bob Marley. Why?"

"I knew it!" I said. "Willy stole it."

"He always does," smiled Kate. She knew exactly what I was talking about.

Over the door, as you enter The Happy Pear café there is a brand new Willyism, written especially for Tao and Mimi ... and it's all Willy's own work, apparently. It says:

Don't worry about a thing because every little thing is going to be all right.

But on the radio, Bob Marley is singing Willy's words to me,

"Don't worry ... 'bout a thing

'Cos every little thing's ... gonna be all right."

And, even though (as usual) Willy had stolen the words, at that moment, they felt exactly right.

My phone shouted, ANSWERMEANSWERME-ANSWERME, which sent Rodent scurrying off Kate's lap and into his cage, which was on the floor. It was a text from Mimi with a photo attached of a newborn baby's wrinkled little face and bald head.

Hi bro. Ur new cuz

Noname. Isnt he
cute? Mimi XXX

I showed it to Kate. She looked at the baby closely.

"It's been a good day, hasn't it, Tao?" she said, and gave me a squeeze.

And I could not remember ever having felt so happy.